Tantalizing Tales

Erotic Sexcapades

Yolanda Williams

Copyright

Table Of Contents

Contact Information

Email: ydw@divayolan.com

Instagram: diva_yolan

Facebook: Diva Yolan

Twitter: Diva_Yolan

Editor: Megan Joseph

Editor Email: Josepheditorialservices@gmail.com

Dedication

To him: you're the inspiration for it all!

Acknowledgements

First and foremost, I give all the honor to God for this gift. I am so appreciative that I am able to follow my passion and bring others some form of entertainment.

Thanks to my family and friends for your continued support and encouragement. Your love, support, and uplifting me keeps me fueled to move forward. I love you all!

To him, and you know who you are, I dedicated this book to you because you are the source behind every word and every story on each page. I appreciate your encouragement to write and send you stories almost every day. I hope you know how much your support has meant to me.

To my readers, I thank you so much for your continued support! If you didn't read, I may not still be writing. I appreciate you more than you will ever know. I hope you continue to enjoy reading my material as I enjoy writing it for you.

This book is going to have you lit in ways one can only imagine. My advice to you is to be near that special one to help put these flames out that are about to be blazing! Smooches!

Part 1: Hot

Chapter 1: Chemistry

Jalisa decided to go study in the science lab since it wasn't her best subject and she needed to study a bit more because she had an exam the following morning. She didn't go to the library as she normally would since she needed the peace and quiet and no disturbances. Too many people would be there and would want to carry on conversations with her. Tonight, just wasn't the night for all of that.

She had just gotten her books out when Professor Walten came in. Professor Eric Walten was a sexy, six-foot-tall, chocolate, bald head brother that looked to be in his mid-twenties but was actually in his late thirties. Every girl and even some guys have all had thoughts of making out with him, and Jalisa definitely had her sights on him. Little did she know though, Professor Walten wanted her just as well.

"Hi there, Miss Langford," he said in his deep baritone voice. He licked his lips as his eyes roamed over her body.

"Hey, Professor. I hope it's okay that I'm in here. I need some extra study time for your exam tomorrow," Jalisa said breathlessly. Just the sight of him got her clit throbbing, and she caught a chill feeling his eyes roam over her body.

"You're doing quite well in my class. I can't imagine you needing extra time to study," Professor Walten said walking over to where she was sitting and taking up the space next to her. The sexual tension between them went from zero to a hundred, real quick.

"Whew! Is it hot in here or is it just me?" Jalisa asked now fanning herself.

"You are definitely hot," he replied lustfully. Jalisa's thong got soaking wet at the comment. Professor Walten leaned in and kissed her on the lips. She happily accepted and returned the kiss. "You have no idea how much I've been wanting to do that," he told her.

"Probably as much as I've been wanting you to do that," she confessed.

Just as she got those words out, Professor Walten had Jalisa on top of the table with her skirt up and thong pulled down. He spread her legs and got in between them, unbuckling his pants. "Are you sure you want to do this before we go any further?" he asked her.

Jalisa ran two of her fingers along her wet pussy and then stuck them in his mouth. "Does that answer your question, Professor?"

No other words were spoken after that. Professor Walten took a seat on the stool Jalisa just occupied then placed her legs over his shoulders. He plummeted his tongue inside her pussy, lapping up her nectar. Jalisa threw her head back enjoying the sensation of his mouth on her. He ate her pussy as if this was his last meal, licking, nibbling, and sucking on her clit. He dipped his tongue in and out of her opening. Jalisa spread her legs wider and pushed his face further in between them. Professor Walten sucked on her clit and fingered the inside of her pussy until he felt her walls contracting from the explosive orgasm he brought her to. "Oooh! Aaaah," Jalisa cried out as she came all over his tongue and face.

After gaining her composure, Jalisa hopped off the table then knelt down between his legs and sucked his dick as if it was the five-star icicle she loved as a child. Taking him into the back of her throat, she swallowed him whole all the while massaging his balls. She pulled it out to the tip and sucked on it, tasting his pre-cum. Feeling how much harder he grew, Jalisa was now ready to be filled by him completely.

She stood, turned her back to him, and positioned herself on his lap. She placed her back to his chest, then eased down onto his hard rod. Taking him inch by inch, Jalisa rode Eric cowgirl style. She placed her hands on the table to steady herself and bounced up and down on his thick dick. Eric played with her nipples as he pumped up inside her, loving the feel of her pussy muscles tightening around his dick with each thrust.

"Ooh. Mmm," Jalisa moaned as she felt her second orgasm taking over her.

For the next two hours they fucked, licked, and sucked on every surface inside that lab. Professor Walten bent her over on his desk, fucked Jalisa up against the wall, she rode his dick while they were on the floor where they both exploded, breaking down the last of the sexual barrier that had been built between them since the beginning of the semester.

"Where do we go from here?" Jalisa asked as they lay on the floor catching their breath. It was evident to her that there was more to this than the mind-blowing sex they'd just had, but she needed to hear him say it.

"Until the semester is over, and you've graduated, we have to keep this on the low," Professor Walten explained.

"That's two weeks away. I can do that," she replied.

"Very good, but in the meantime let's take this back to my place so I can help you study for my exam you have tomorrow," He said seductively helping Jalisa off the floor.

They began putting their clothes on when Larry, the maintenance guy, walked in on them. Needless to say, this was a Kodak moment of the looks plastered on each of their faces. But Larry played it off and moved about the lab as if they were not there. Jalisa and Professor Walten quickly dressed and exited the lab.

Two weeks later....

Jalisa showed the last of her family and friends out of the house after a celebratory-filled day for her graduating from college. She busied herself around the house tidying up the place. She had just put the last of the dishes in the dishwasher when her phone rang. Looking at the caller ID and seeing Eric Walten's name, Jalisa perked up.

"Hello," she cooed through the speaker.

"Hello to you, Miss Graduate," Eric seductively replied.

"I like the sound of that!" She smiled while twirling a strand of her hair around a finger. She sat in the chair with her legs dangling over the arm. She was excited because tonight had finally come where she and Eric would finally reconnect since their rendezvous in the lab.

"Are you ready for me?"

"Ready and wet. Are you on your way?"

"Damn, I like the sound of that, and I'll be there in about thirty minutes. I'm coming from across town." Eric, too, was excited about tonight. He had his eyes on Jalisa from the moment he saw her. She was a freshman at the time, walking down the hall on her way to class. He was turned on by her innocent girl next door look, glasses and all. He could tell underneath the baggy jeans and oversized hoodie, there was a banging, curvaceous body. But more than that, there was something about her that took ahold of him. Watching her saunter down the hallway and into a classroom, he vowed right then and there he would have her.

"I can't wait to see you. I'm gonna go freshen up and I'll see you when you get here," Jalisa told him.

"Cool. I'll see you in a few."

They disconnected the call and Jalisa jumped up and ran into her bedroom. She went into her master bathroom and turned on the shower. As she gave the water time to heat up to her desired temperature, she rushed back into her bedroom and over to her dresser drawer where she pulled out the Victoria's Secret royal blue teddy and matching thong she bought just for this occasion. She quickly showered, dressed, and scented her body with Ralph Lauren's Romance.

By the time Jalisa lit scented candles throughout the house, turned on some music to set the mood, and poured a glass of wine, the doorbell chimed. She opened the door and gasped at the sight that stood before her. Standing before her was the tall glass of dark chocolate in the form of Eric Walten. Wearing a pair of crisp black jeans, black t-shirt that fit like a glove, and J's, Eric smiled a set of pearly whites holding a bag of take-out in one hand and a bottle of wine in the other.

"Hello to you, too," Eric said as he roamed Jalisa's body from head to toe. He was aroused at seeing the royal blue lingerie against her coco brown skin. The cups lifted her perky B-cup breasts, and the sheer fabric flowed down just enough to cover her ample bottom. His manhood pulsated against his zipper as he watched her turn and walk into the living room. He closed the door behind him, then followed her inside to the living room.

"Thanks for the food, but that's not what I'm hungry for," Jalisa said. She stood in the middle of the living room with her hands on her hips and tilted her head to the side.

"Oh really? Well, tell me, Ms. Langford, exactly what are you hungry for?" Eric asked as he sat the bags on the coffee table. He stood in front of her then cupped a breast. Her nipples immediately hardened at his touch.

Jalisa grabbed the back of Eric's head and pulled him in for a kiss. He wrapped his arms around her waist, grabbing her bodacious ass in the process. Their tongues did an intimate dance with each other, starting off slow, then becoming more aggressive. Jalisa moaned in Eric's mouth giving more access to her tongue, suckling on it with passion. They began removing each other's clothing piece by piece until they were both naked. For several moments they both stood admiring each other's bodies.

She knelt down in front of him at eye level to his dick. With her legs spread apart giving him a full view of her wet pussy, Jalisa sucked his dick into her mouth without using her hands. He hissed when she deep throated him. She moaned feeling the tip of his dick hitting the back of her throat. This sent shock waves down his dick and to his toes. Eric grabbed the back of her head and slowly began pumping in and out of her mouth. Jalisa obliged him circling her tongue around his shaft. She grabbed his balls and massaged them gently with one hand while playing in her pussy with the other.

"Aah, ssss, mmmm," Eric moaned in pleasure as Jalisa tugged on his ball sack. She looked up at him and winked. Eric exploded right then in her mouth, emptying what felt like a bucket load down her throat. Jalisa swallowed every drop.

She stood, grabbed his hand, and led him to the sofa. The bedroom was too far for her at the moment. She was wet and ready to be filled by him. Being that she anticipated that to happen, she had already lined the sofa with a blanket. Laying on the sofa, Jalisa spread eagle, placing one leg over the back and the other she held out to the side. Eric marveled by the site of the prettiest pussy he'd ever seen. It glistened from her wetness as she went back to playing with herself. He went to kneel down to get a taste, but Jalisa stopped him. "Nah, I want that dick in me right now."

"Well alright," he crooned climbing between her thighs.

16

She took the fingers out of her pussy and placed them to his lips. He opened his mouth and sucked her juices off them before leaning down and kissing her. He entered her in one thrust and the both gasped at the connection. Jalisa began grinding her pelvis back and forth on Eric, fucking him from the bottom. He got in tune with her rhythm and stroked long and hard, hitting her walls from every angle. Jalisa pressed her head in the arm of the sofa as she arched her back when she felt him hitting her spot. Eric pushed her legs further apart as he thrust faster pushing her love button. Jalisa grabbed his ass cheeks and pulled him into her further as they swayed to their own music of pleasure.

"Eric! Oh, baby, fuck this pussy!" Jalisa moaned in ecstasy.

Seeing she was close to an orgasm, Eric pulled out and rubbed the head of his dick along the folds of her pussy. He grinned deviously at her knowing she wanted him to finish her off. He wanted to see how long she could hold out. "What are you doing? Put it back in!" Jalisa demanded.

"I don't want you to come yet," he told her. He continued to rub his dick along her folds then quickly thrust back inside her.

"Aaaahhh!" Jalisa screamed out in pleasure.

Eric moaned feeling how hard her walls contracted around him gripping him harder with each thrust. Every thrust he made, the stronger her walls clamped around him. He found her g-spot again and began his interrogation on it, pounding hard into it then teasing it with a light brush. Jalisa yelled out obscenities for him to stop playing with her and fuck her already. He groaned out a chuckle as her legs began shaking and her breathing was like a woman practicing Lamaze.

"Oh shit! I'm coming! I'm coming!" Jalisa shouted. Her pussy muscles locked Eric in place as she creamed all over his dick. She caused him to shoot his sperm inside of her with the death grip her pussy had on his dick.

"Shit, Ja-lisa! Damn!" Eric belted as they climaxed together.

He released her legs and laid on top of her, catching his breath and waiting for her muscles to relax around him. Eric couldn't believe the power of the pussy until that day. Never in his life since he'd been sexually active had a woman ever gripped his dick the way Jalisa had done. The thought of that was making his dick hard again and soon they were back at it.

He pulled out and knelt down to taste her brown sugar. Not only did Jalisa have the prettiest pussy he'd ever seen, but she tasted the sweetest. Most women's pussies he'd had the pleasure of tasting, were on the salty side. But Jalisa's pussy was blander or clean tasting to him with a hint of brown sugar. Even now after they had explosive orgasms and with the mixture of their fluids, she still tasted like brown sugar.

He reveled in her cave, lapping, licking, nibbling, and enjoying the taste, feel, and smell of her. He licked his way down to her ass and stroked his tongue back and forth and around her anus. Jalisa jolted off the sofa from his surprise attack. He licked her ass the same as he licked her pussy. He inserted three fingers inside her pussy and massaged her inner walls as his tongue played with her ass.

"Oh my, Eric!"

"Every part of you tastes so sweet," Eric said in between licks. "Mmm, so good."

When he stuck his tongue inside her asshole, Jalisa's body jerked in pleasure and she squirted as she came. Eric positioned his dick at her asshole and slid in with ease. Jalisa cried out from the pain and pleasure sensation she was experiencing. She had never had backdoor play and was taken aback by Eric's move. However, she couldn't deny that it felt good. It was a sensation she'd never felt from vaginal penetration. It was an indescribable feeling she didn't want him to stop giving her.

Once she completely relaxed and got into his rhythm, she found herself playing with her clit, heightening the feeling of pleasure. Eric enjoyed watching her play in her pussy as he thrust in and out of her ass. This made his dick harder and they both moaned in pleasure they both were coming together. Jalisa felt pure essence as her orgasm burst through her ass to her pussy and out of her body like the fourth of July fireworks. She circled her clit faster as she came so hard, she damn near passed out. Eric bust his nut inside her ass and he too felt the fireworks as he emptied himself.

He pulled out of her and fell back onto the sofa. There they fell asleep from the blissful chemistry that took over them.

Chapter 2: That Night

After several months of texting and conversing over the phone, he invited me over to his place. I immediately became nervous, excited, and horny all at the same time. I had just gotten out of the shower when my cell phone chimed his special notification tone. I read his message and responded to let him know I was on my way. I scrambled around my bedroom trying to figure out what I was going to wear and packing a bag all at the same time. I got dressed and got on the freeway only to come to a halt due to an accident. Sitting at a standstill, I thought back to the night we had sex for the first time.

It was one night after leaving a masquerade dance his fraternity throws every year. I wore a red, knee-length haltered dress. It was sequenced but not too shiny though. And it fit my curvy frame perfectly. I felt like a celebrity because all eyes were on me as I strutted up to the entrance of the venue. Several of the distinct men of the fraternity greeted me just outside the door, each placing a set of beads around my neck. He was the last to place a bead around my neck. He gave me a hug and whispered in my ear "You're going home with me tonight."

My response was, "We'll see," I flashed him a smile then proceeded inside. I took the steps leading up to the ballroom where the festivities took place. 'Hellos' and 'Damn she fine' were thrown my way as I sashayed by several gentlemen.

It was packed and the dance was all the way live! There was a band on stage performing live. A buffet style set up of finger food, pasta salad, fresh fruit, and wings aligned both sides of the ballroom. The bar set off to the left of the room and had a line of patrons waiting to get a shot of tequila or a glass of Hennessey and coke. I walked around for a bit looking for a few associates from work who said they would be in attendance. I finally found them sitting at one of the round tables right by the dance floor. I joined them at the table and began to get my party on.

A couple of hours later he found me sitting at the table eating and took a seat in the empty chair beside me. He ran a hand down my leg and then said, "Damn your legs are so smooth and shiny," I could only smile and nod my head since I had a mouthful of food. "Are you gonna come home with me?" He asked me.

I took a sip of my vodka and cranberry drink before I said, "Yes."

"I'll be leaving in a few minutes because I have a paper due," he told me.

"I am, too. I have to work in the morning so I'm gonna go home, pack a bag, and then head to you. I'll be closer to the job at your place anyway."

"Ok. Let me know when you leave out."

"Alright," he left and mingled for a few minutes while I finished off my plate of food and drink.

I said my goodbyes and headed home to gather my things. I had small talk with my roommate while I packed letting her know I was out for the night. It was around 1:30 in the morning when I made it to his apartment. He gave me a hug as soon as I crossed the threshold. I took in the décor of black and gold accentuating the living room-dining room combo. I was pleasantly surprised as to how large, neat, and clean it was. I followed him into the bedroom that donned a large high post king sized bed. I sat my bag down and gave him my work uniform to hang up.

"The bathroom is right there," he told me pointing to the door just outside of the bedroom.

"Okay, I'm going to take a shower," I announced. I went into the bathroom and handled my business. When I came out, I had on a pair of boy shorts and a tank top. He was in the bed and had to assist me into it because it sat so high. I snuggled up next to him and our hands immediately began roaming each other's bodies. My hand snaked inside his boxers and wrapped around his pole that grew hard to my touch. I gave the tip a squeeze before stroking from the tip to the base.

He lifted my tank top and latched on to a nipple, sucking on it as he squeezed the other. A moan escaped from the pleasure his tongue was giving my hardened nipples. He pulled the tank top over my head and pulled my boy shorts off. He then pulled his boxers off, ripped the foil off the condom, and roll it down his big dick. "I want to ride it," I announced and crawled on top of him. I aligned the head with my opening and eased down until he filled me completely. I had to sit on it a minute to get adjusted to his size. I began a slow grind riding him as his sausage seemed to grow even larger with every stroke.

Picking up the pace we matched each other stroke for stroke. I could feel my juices flowing down onto his dick as I squeezed my pussy muscles on him. All of a sudden, he flipped me on my back and was on top of me with my legs in the air, never breaking contact! Well damn! He thrust hard and deep inside my tunnel. "Ooh shit," I shouted as I came. He continued to thrust hard and deep, hitting my spot until he exploded in the condom and my legs shook from my second orgasm.

My pussy muscles contracted as he pulled out of me. Once he was off of me, I had to cross my legs to try and calm the contractions that were still pulsating. I shook my head at this get down with a huge Kool-Aid smile plastered on my face. After laying eyes on this man three years ago along with conversations over the phone and emailing back and forth, here I was lying in his bed after some amazing sex. If I didn't have to be up in a few hours I wouldn't have mind going for round two. He came out of the bathroom and put his boxers on. He then helped me out of bed, and I went into the bathroom and took another shower. I redressed and he helped me back in bed again. I set the alarm on my phone and snuggled up with him before falling to sleep in his arms.

The alarm sounded at 5:15 a.m. waking me out of a peaceful slumber. I honestly did not want to move out of the comfortable position I laid in. I unwrapped myself out of his embrace and reluctantly slid out of bed and got dressed for work. I woke him to let him know I was about to leave, and we hugged for a minute before breaking our embrace. I stepped out to the cold and rain hitting my face, but I didn't care one bit. I headed to work with thoughts of that previous night or more so the hours before and just couldn't take that big smile off my face. It was that night that had me walking around the next day announcing to everyone I encountered that it was a beautiful day, although in actuality it was cold, wet, and gloomy.

I was brought back to the present by the sounds of car horns honking for the cars to begin moving. Finally, after an hour at a standstill the traffic began to move. I called him to let him know what was going on and that I was still on my way. It was two hours after his invite that I'm greeted by him at his door. Butterflies filled my stomach and nervousness took over me as we embraced for a hug.

"What are you doing up in here?" I asked him, sitting my bag in one of the chairs at the dining table. I took my coat off and slung it across the same chair.

"Filling out this job application," he told me as he took a seat on the sectional where he had his laptop sitting. I sat down beside him and took in the décor of the apartment. It was a typical bachelor pad with a red leather sectional, large flat screen television, and a round wood table with four matching chairs that took up the living room dining room combo. Scented candles burned giving the apartment a sweet fruity smell.

I took my boots off then took a seat on the sectional next to him. Butterflies continued to dance around in my belly as I tried to make myself comfortable. I watched on as he continued to fill out the job application and we chatted all the while. "Olympus Has Fallen" had come on no sooner than I sat down. I tucked my feet underneath me and got comfortable as I watched the movie. I was so enthralled in it that he had finished the job application and shutting down his laptop.

"Well, sweetheart, I have to hit it in the morning so I'm about to turn in," he told me as he stood up. I wanted to finish the movie, so I told him I'd join him when it went off. He left me on the sectional and went into his bedroom which was situated just off the kitchen area.

The movie ended about fifteen minutes later and I sauntered into the pitch-black bedroom after turning off the television and lights. I undressed down to my panty and bra set before getting his assistance into the extremely high king-sized bed. It was like déjà vu all over again as I snuggled up to him. I laid with my back against his chest and my big booty pressed against his large dick. He wrapped his arm around my waist, pulling me closer to him before grabbing my breast. I grinded my ass on him and could feel him getting hard. I turned so that I was facing him, and he undid my bra, pulling it off and tossing it somewhere onto the floor.

I placed my hand inside of his boxer briefs and wrapped it around his dick which was rock hard by now. He latched on to my breast, sucking on it. Just as our fourplay was picking up, he leaned over and grabbed a condom off the nightstand. Precum oozed out of the tip and I rubbed it around the head with my thumb before licking the remains off. When I heard him tear the condom pack open, I pulled my panties off and tossed them on the floor. I laid back and opened my legs to accept him in between them.

He pushed my legs open wider and placed the tip at my opening. He then latched back on to one of my breasts as he thrust inside of me. I gasped at the pain and pleasure of his entrance. He continued to suck on my breast as he slow grind in me. I threw the pussy back matching him stroke for stroke. It got so good to me that I lifted one of my legs up and over my head and pulled him deeper inside me.

He placed my leg in the crook of his arm as he continued to slow stroke my pussy hitting my spot. I moaned in pleasure as I nibbled on his ear and kissed his neck. He then positioned himself to where my left leg was resting on his left shoulder as he continued to show no mercy on my g-spot. My vaginal walls began to contract from this positioned as he fucked me bringing me to an orgasm. Not letting up on the ride he was taking me on, he flipped me over without pulling out of me and had me on all fours, hitting my pussy from the back. He thrust hard inside of me pushing me all the way into the bed. Picking up the pace with his strokes, I moaned louder with pleasure, popping my pussy on his dick.

"You gonna make me cum in this pussy!" He let out. "Oh, I'm about to cum in this pussy!" He said and came inside the condom. My pussy contracted from the orgasm I had along with him as he deflated inside the condom. He pulled out of me and all I could do was just lay there and allow my contractions to subside. He smacked me on my ass as he climbed out of bed and went into the bathroom.

By the time he came out of the bathroom, my contractions had stopped, and my breathing was back to normal. He placed his boxer briefs back on as I climbed out of bed and went into the bathroom. It was then I realized he had slow jams playing on his iPod while we were getting it on. I grabbed a couple of towels out of the closet he'd pointed out to me when I came into the bathroom and took a shower. After washing up, I joined him back in bed and snuggled under him before falling asleep. Sometime later I woke up and felt his hand on my ass. "Are you okay?" I was shocked to hear him say.

"Yes, I'm fine," I told him.

"Is it too hot in here for you? If so, I can turn the heat down some," he said.

"No, it feels really good in here," I explained and pulled the covers up around my neck getting back into the comfortable position I was in next to him. He rubbed my ass once more before he turned away and fell back to sleep.

At 5:15 a.m. his alarm went off, letting us both know it was time to get the day started. He silenced the alarm and reluctantly got out of bed and went into the bathroom. I lay there not wanting to move from under the comfort of the warm covers. I eventually climbed out of bed and put on my clothes. I watched him and made small talk as he got dressed for work. He chose a pair of navy-blue pants, striped shirt, and some brown loafers out of the massive wardrobe in his walk-in closet. He had more clothes and shoes than me, and I have a huge wardrobe!

After he got dressed and grabbed himself something for his lunch, he set the alarm to his apartment as we exited. We hugged and he gave me a kiss as we said our goodbyes and went our separate ways. I made my way to I-75 heading south, merging into the morning rush hour traffic with a smile on my face and gleam in my eyes as I played that night over in my mind.

Chapter 3: The Quickie

He moved my panties to the side and slid right in. I gasped at the size of him trying to push his way through my tunnel. I spread my legs wider welcoming him in further. We got into a rhythm as I matched him stroke for stroke. Sounds of pleasure invaded the walls of the bathroom we were in for this quickie. Going faster and deeper, he caused a loud moan to escape me just before he snaked his tongue into my mouth. I wrapped my legs around his waist and began bouncing on his large dick. Finding my g-spot he strokes harder as I continued to bounce my juicy pussy on his massive dick. I could feel my orgasm coming on and my legs began to shake. I threw my head back against the mirror and arched my back. He fucked me faster and harder as we both climaxed together.

We got ourselves back into presentable form and exited the bathroom, he goes left and I went right making my way back to the party. We were at my friend Renee's housewarming party and needless to say he and I christened her guest bathroom for her!

Renee was such a socialite and everyone who was anyone had come to show her some love. I was not going to come out tonight but after being cursed out from here to Sunday by Renee, I changed my mind. I had a hectic day and really just wanted to snuggle up on my sofa and binge watch my recorded shows. But knowing how dramatic Renee would act if I was a no show after she ripped me a new asshole over the phone, here I am four hours later.

As soon as I crossed the threshold into the foyer, our eyes met. He was looking oh so fine wearing a pair of black loose-fitting jeans with a black sweater. His hair cut low and nicely trimmed goatee outlined the sexiest smile I'd ever seen. He looked like he stood about six-foot-two with just the right amount of muscles bulging through the arms of the sweater.

It was him! The guy from work earlier today. I wonder how he knows Renee. Up until today I had never seen him before. I work at one of the largest law firms in town, the law office of Steinbrook and Daniels and he came in this morning seeking representation. He was what made my day so hectic!

So, I'm up for promotion to become junior partner and am the only female to ever be considered. I'm competing against Perter Steinbrook's son Thomas and another colleague Drexil Standford. I'm the underdog in this competition and for obvious reasons. I didn't grow up with a silver spoon in my mouth like they did. Everything I have I worked extra hard for. From high school through college and on to law school, I was faced with "You won't make," or "You can't do that," all coming from my mother. She despised me because I look so much like the man who knocked her up at the age of sixteen and left her to be a single, teen mom. I had to prove to her and everyone else that told me I couldn't do something or that I'd be nothing, they had me all the way fucked up.

I was valedictorian of my high school, college, and law school graduating classes. I came out of law school with six job offers across the country and three from overseas. I chose Steinbrook and Daniels since they were located in New York, the contract offer was the best, and because I knew working here would be my biggest challenge yet. They had a reputation for not hiring many female lawyers. So, when I got the job offer, I knew then I could do anything I set my mind to.

Anyway, Mr. Daniels called Drexil, Thomas, and I into the conference room to meet with a potential client. Him. We were all seated around the large mahogany conference table making small talk when he walked in commanding everyone's attention without saying a word. The sight of him immediately made my panties moist.

"Gentlemen and Lydia, I want you all to meet Michael Spencer. He wants to come on as a client and he agreed to let you all use him as your case for the junior partnership challenge." Mr. Daniels announced. "Mr. Spencer—"

"Please call me Mike," he said in a deep sultry baritone. I swear I came right then and there.

"Correction, Mike will sit with each of you so you can discuss his needs and wants with the firm and then you will pitch your case to David and me later today."

Wait, what?! How in the hell am I gonna be able to sit with all of that fine-ness in close proximity and maintain control?! All of a sudden, I couldn't breathe, and I started hyperventilating. "Lydia are you alright?" I hear Thomas ask but I couldn't respond. I began fanning myself with some of the folders I'd brought with me to the meeting.

"Call down to Dr. Morgan's office and have him come up asap," Mr. Daniels barked to no one in particular.

"No, please don't!" I yelled. "I'm okay, just a little asthma attack but I'm okay. Just need some air," I explained trying to get myself together while fanning myself at the same time. How embarrassing is it to have an episode in front of your boss and a potential client?! Uugghh! I wanted to scream out.

"Are you sure we don't need to call him?" Thomas asked with a smirk I wanted to slap off his face.

"I'm sure. Please excuse me while I go to the lady's room," I stood on wobbly legs for a few seconds before exiting the office.

Bursting through the door to the restroom, I rushed over to one of the sinks and ran some cold water. I dashed a handful on my face to cool down. I grabbed some paper towels and dried my face off. "What the hell is wrong with you? Get your shit together, Lydia!" I said to my reflection in the mirror.

"Here you go," my assistant, Stephanie, said holding my purse out for me. I didn't even hear her come in.

"Thanks," I took my purse from her and took out my makeup bag. We were silence as I reapplied makeup that really wasn't needed to my face. "How do I look?" I turned to face Stephanie.

"Gorgeous as always."

"Thanks," I sighed.

"Hey you got this. Just go in there and do what you always do," she encouraged.

"Step, it's something about this man that has me off my square. I can't get my mind right," I said in a low whisper.

"You're going to have to look pass all of the sexiness he's exuding and handle your business if you want this promotion!" Step fussed at me.

"I know that, but it ain't stopping what I'm feeling. This is something I can't explain nor understand right now."

"Ah, chile, that ain't nothing but lust and the need to get laid," she waved her hand in the air like she was shooing a fly away. "Hell, how long has it been for you anyway?" She chuckled.

"This isn't funny, Stephanie!" I explained trying to sound serious but ended up laughing along with her. She always knows what to say and do to get me back on track, even if it was something crazy. Although Stephanie is my assistant, she's also one of my closest friends. She knows how to get me all the way together when needed and I'm grateful for her. "Okay let's do this," I said to her and we head out of the restroom.

"Lydia, are you alright now?" Mr. Daniels asked with sincere concern as soon as I stepped back into the conference room. Walking to my seat I could feel all eyes on me.

"Yes, I'm fine," I smiled and took my seat which was next to Mike. I crossed my legs and put on my no nonsense, let's get down to business look. Mr. Daniels smiled and continued with the meeting.

Mike was to meet with Thomas first, then Drexil, and I was last. Our meeting was at one this afternoon which was normally my lunch time. However, I was too nervous about this meeting to eat so I worked on a few cases that were pending. At 12:55, Stephanie informed me Mike was waiting for me and I had her escort him in. I gave myself a pep talk and prayed this meeting wouldn't take long.

Stephanie knocked on the door then opened it wide for Mike's entrance. "Good afternoon Mr. Spencer," I stood and walked around to the other side of my desk extending my hand out for him to shake.

"Hello Ms. McCoy," he said taking my hand into his giving it a firm shake. I tried to pull away, but he held into my hand. We stood there momentarily gazing into each other's eyes.

"May I have my hand back?" I asked. Flashing me that sexy smile Mike released my hand and took a seat in one of the chairs that sat at my desk.

Stephanie shook her head at the scene that played out before her as she closed the door. I sashayed back to my seat and sat across from Mike. "How's your day going so far?" I asked pulling up my computer screen and retrieving my files with his information.

"So far everything's going well. Time seemed to have passed so quickly though, with all of these meetings this morning that I haven't had lunch yet. Before I knew it, it was time for our meeting," he said.

"Yes, same here. I'll make this quick and then you can go on about your day. So, let's get started," I was about to go over the information when he interrupted me.

"How about we go over this while having lunch? I'm hungry and you are too, so let's go eat and discuss this on full stomachs. What you say?"

"I'd prefer if we can get this over with," I said hoping he'd agree. I was having trouble keeping my composure around him. I just wanted this done and over with.

"Yes, but I'm the client and I say we go eat."

He stood towering over me. I could feel my juices trickling down and had to cross my legs to calm my pulsating clit. I have been pursued by some very wealthy and powerful men, good looking men, but they have never had a pull on me like the man that stood before me and it was scaring the hell out of me. How can someone you've never met before make you feel this way at first sight? Several of my girlfriends have talked about this before and I just thought they were full of shit. That was until today.

"You feel it too, huh?" Mike asked breaking my thoughts.

"Wha... what you say?" I asked dumbly.

"I said you feel it too."

"Feel what exactly?"

"I felt it the moment I spotted you hopping into a cab on 125th a few months ago. You were wearing a navy-blue skirt with a white blouse showing off your amazing figure. Your hair was pulled back into a bun.

And I said, 'wow she the most beautiful woman I have ever seen'," Mike explained. He walked around to my side of the desk and sat in the edge of it. "I knew then I had to have you. So, I did some research, called around to some people, to find out whatever I could about you. It took a minute, but I found you," he said in a low tone. I was speechless. I honestly was at a loss for words.

I thought back to that day, the day I ended my last relationship or more so a situationship. It was one of those relationships that was for convenience, that was until the guy wanted to take things to the next level. I wasn't ready or more so that I just knew Lance wasn't the one I wanted to settle down with. He wanted me to marry him and become a housewife. I laughed in his face and told him to kiss my ass because me becoming anyone's housewife will never happen. I worked too damn hard to get this far in my career to be a housewife. And for him to even think I would accept that told me Lance never really knew me at all, or that he didn't care. So, that day was our last rendezvous, a farewell fuck fest since I knew it would be a while before I got some.

The ringing of my phone brought me out of my trance. "Yes, Stephanie," I said staring into Mike's dark brown eyes. He licked his lips and my breath caught in my throat. Seeing that got my nipples so hard that they began to hurt. He smoothly pulled me between his legs and wrapped his arm around my waist.

"Randy just called and said there's a car waiting for you and Mr. Spencer?" She more so asked than commented. I tried to keep my attention to what she was saying but was having a hard time with Mike placing light kisses in the crook of my neck. He eased a hand up my dress and slid a finger through the side of my panties and into my wetness.

"Y-yes, Mr. Spencer wants to have this meeting over lunch. Let him know we will be down momentarily," I told her. I tried to my best to hold in the moan that wanted to escape my mouth. Mike slowly thrust his finger in and out my pulsating pussy. Holding the phone tightly in my hand, I looked into his eyes and I knew then he was one of those men who thought the world revolves around them. I was immediately turned off.

"Yes ma'am," she said before disconnecting the call.

I hung up the phone and pulled away from him. "So, there's a car waiting for us downstairs," I said to Mike with a raised eyebrow.

"I told you I was hungry and wanted to have this meeting over lunch. Let's go," he demanded making his way toward the door. As he waited for me, he placed the finger that was just inside of me up to his nose and sniffed. He closed his eyes as he took in my scent before placing his finger in his mouth and sucking my juices off.

Sighing, I reluctantly locked my computer, grabbed my files, and placed them in my briefcase. I removed my suit jacket from my chair then put it on. "Let's go," I mumbled. My legs felt like noodles as I walked toward him. My pussy contracted with each step I took. Mike shook his head and chuckled as we left the office.

"Stephanie, clear my schedule for the rest of the day. After lunch I'll be heading home. Once you're done you can go as well," I told her. Stephanie gave me a concerned look since it's very rare that I would leave work so early. I'm usually the first one in and the last to leave.

36

"Uh, yes ma'am." Stephanie responded.

Mike took me to an upscale restaurant over on 119th and Lennox. The decor was nice with several crystal chandeliers hanging throughout, crisp white linen tablecloths over the tables, with an array of fresh bouquet of flowers on each table. A grand piano sat smack in the middle of the restaurant and was being played by an older white man who resembled the cartoon character Mr. Magoo.

Mike must frequent this place a lot because the hostess greeted him by name as soon as we walked in and escorted us to a table. "Carmen will be your server today and she'll be with you in a few moments. Can I go ahead and get you something to drink while you wait?" The hostess was eyeing him like she wanted to get naked right then and there for him.

"Bring us a bottle of Domaine de la Romanee-Conti," he stated smoothly.

"Yes, sir."

Carmen, the waitress, came over a few minutes later with the bottle of wine and two long stem wine glasses. She took our order and I got down to business as soon as she walked away. Well, I tried to get right to the business at hand. "Mr. Spencer, why do you want Steinbrook and Daniels to represent you?" I asked him.

He ignored my question as he poured wine into each of our glasses. Instead of answering my question, he asked "Are you seeing anyone?"

"My personal business is none of your business and has nothing to do with this meeting," I was starting to get agitated with him and his arrogance. "Can you answer my question please?"

"It doesn't matter either way because I'm going to make you mine. I just want to know if I need to remove someone who may be in the way." Mike continued as if I never said a mumbling word. "Lydia, I'm a, man who sees what he wants, goes after it, and get it. And right now, I'm on a mission to get you," I started to speak but he put his hand up to stop me. "I'm not done."

The nerve of this pompous ass! Who does he think he is?! If he thinks I'm going to be that easy, he got another thing coming! I'm trying my best to not go ape shit on his ass right now because of what's at stake, but I'm about two New York seconds away from going the fuck off! My leg began to shake, a habit I picked up as a child whenever my mom pissed me off. Being out in public and in this nice restaurant is the only reason I'm maintaining some class about myself right about now. So, I pick up my wine glass and take a large gulp while giving Mr. Spencer the evil eye.

"There's no need in fighting this when you know you want me just as much as I want you. Even now with you sitting there mean mugging me, I know you're turned on by all of this. I know I am," he taunted tilting his head to the side smirking. "Tell me Lydia, am I lying? Hmm? Tell me you didn't like the way I played in your pussy back at your office. Hmm?"

My heart felt like it was about to explode, it was beating so hard and fast. I wanted to scream 'hell yes you're lying' but I couldn't form the words. All I could do was lower my head and fidget with my cloth napkin. My mind was saying no but my body was on a whole other level. It was confusing to want to smack the shit out of this man but want him to smack my ass at the same damn time. I've worked in some of the toughest cases ever, but this by far was one of the toughest things I've had to deal with.

"Mr. Spencer, it would be a lie if I was to say I'm not attracted to you. But if you think I'm just going to lay on my back and let you have your way with me when I know absolutely nothing about you, not to mention you're an arrogant ass, well you're out of your damn mind," I stood and gathered my things. "When you're ready to continue this meeting on a professional level, call my office and set up an appointment with my assistant. Until then stay away from me," I walked out before he had a chance to respond.

Now you see how hectic my day was. I didn't get to complete my presentation today and the bosses came down on me hard about it too. I gave them a bullshit story and promised to have it resolved next week.

I made my way through the crowd to where Renee was in a deep conversation with our friend Chanel. The three of us met in college at a frat party and have been thick as thieves ever since. "I'm so glad you made it! You know I was gonna come to your place and kick your ass if you hadn't come," Renee proclaimed as she hugged me.

"Yes, I know. I hate I came though!" I said.

"Why?" Chanel asked.

"Yeah, why? I'm one of your best friends and you don't want to help me celebrate this new chapter of my life? What the hell, Lydia?" Renee said being dramatic as usual.

"No, Renee, that's not it! You know I'm not like that so why are you getting extra with me?" Renee just didn't know this was not the time for her antics.

"Then tell me what it is," she snarled.

"If you calm your ass down, I will. Damn!" Seeing she was really pissing me off, Chanel diffused the situation and I told them about what happened at work.

"Damn, Lyd, I'm sorry to hear that. So, what are you going to do being you're up for this promotion?" Chanel asked.

"I don't know but I have to figure it out before Monday." A server came by with wine glasses and I grabbed two off the tray and gulped them both down.

"Drinking is not going to solve your problems," Renee said snatching the glasses out of my hands. She looked at me in disgust before walking away.

"Seriously, Renee?" I huffed.

Chanel waved her off. "Let her go. You know how she feels about us drinking after what happened that one time."

"I know but my problems are more important than a damn housewarming party!" I snapped.

Chanel shook her head, "Maybe so but you know she needs this after everything Rob put her through. She's trying to start over with her life and as one of her best friends you should be supportive of this."

"I am supportive of her, Chanel. All I'm saying is that I have major issues of my own right now. Getting this promotion is very important to me so why not support me right now." They're acting like I'm never there for them when I'm always first to their side in their time of need. This one time I need some support and I get nothing.

"You have my support and Renee's, Lyd. But tonight, is her night so can you put your problems to the side and let's celebrate our friend?" Chanel asked. She bumped shoulders with me and gave me that sad, puppy dog look she'd give when she wanted something. I rolled my eyes at her and she squealed, giving me a hug because she knew I'd given in.

"Whatever. Get the hell off me," I playfully pushed her off me.

For the next couple of hours, I mingled with the guest avoiding Mike the entire time. I didn't tell the girls it was him I was talking about because they would have made a scene, and I didn't want that to happen. I made my way outside on the patio and sat on the steps. It was a clear and warm night. You can see the stars twinkling in the sky. The air was so crisp and refreshing. The party was in full effect, but I wasn't. I wanted to be home with my remote control in one hand and a spoon to dip into my cookies and cream ice cream in the other.

"Ten more minutes and I'm out," I said aloud to myself.

"The party is just getting started," he said startling me. I gasped and placed my hand on my chest, turning to face Mike.

"You scared the crap out of me," I said once I was able to speak.

"I'm sorry. I wasn't trying to do that. I saw you come out here and just came to check on you." Mike said.

"I was fine until you showed up. So, can you go now? I want to be alone."

"No one wants to be alone, Lydia." Mike said. He then came and took a seat next to me on the steps.

"Well right now I do. Why are you even here? How do you know Renee anyway?"

"My son attends her school."

"Oh, so you have a son? What's his name?"

"Yep. His name is Alex. He's a good kid. He's just been acting out a lot since his mom passed away," Mike explained.

"Oh no. I'm so sorry to hear that," I said sympathetically.

"It's okay. She had cancer that was progressive and there was nothing the doctors could do. He's just too young to understand right now. All he knows is that his mommy is sleeping. And it's keeping him awake at night because he keeps having nightmares and calling for her."

"Give him warm milk before bed. That always helped my sister when we were kids. She had nightmares a lot and I would give her warm milk."

"Thanks. I'll try that."

We sat in silence after that, each of us lost in our own thoughts. Mike sat forward with his elbows resting on his thighs and I was leaning back onto my elbows. This was surprisingly pleasant watching the stars.

Laughter with the mixture of the music and various conversations going on at the same time, resonated from inside.

"It's getting late. I'm about to head home," I announced as I sat up. Mike stood up and held out a hand to help me up. I grabbed his hand and stood up. We were now face to face. Before I knew it, we were kissing, softly then with so much passion, we appeared to be long lost lovers, lovers who were suddenly taken away from each other but somehow found their way back.

Realizing what we... I was doing, I pulled away from Mike. We stood there staring at each other with flames of passion burning in our eyes. Our chests moving up and down as we try to catch our breaths. It's no doubt that there is a sexual chemistry brewing between us that is about to spill over any minute now. But I cannot cross that line. It will be unethical and dangerous. This could ruin my career.

"Good night Mr. Spencer," I said and left him standing on the porch.

I went back inside and headed straight to the guest bathroom. As soon as I was inside, I locked the door and leaned against it. I pulled my skirt up and slid two fingers inside my wet tunnel. I was so wet and horny that there was no way I could drive home without releasing this orgasm that I have to get off.

A knock on the door interrupted my intimate time. "Just a minute," I let out still playing with myself.

There was another knock on the door. Whoever was knocking was being rude and impatient. I decided I'd just have to wait until I got in my car since the windows are tinted. I used the bathroom and then washed myself and my hands off. I opened the door to see Mike standing there. I tried to move past him, but he shoved me back into the bathroom then closed and locked it behind him.

"What are you doing?" I asked.

"Finishing what we started," Mike replied as he picked me up and placed me onto the counter. He pushed my skirt up over my butt as I undid his pants and pulled out the biggest and prettiest dick I had ever seen. Well you already know what happened next.

Chapter 4: Him

For as long as I can remember, I've always been a sexual being. At a very early age, I learned friction to my private area made me feel good. And when I learned that a boy sticking his thing inside my private area gave me that very same feeling, I couldn't wait to have it done to me. But it wasn't until I turned twenty-five, that I finally got to experience real sex with a man for the first time. And let me tell y'all, it pissed me off! Before then, though I have experienced getting my pussy eaten and I've even given blow jobs but getting dicked down never happened. Why, you ask? I'll get to that in a moment. But check it....

I don't know which pissed me off the most: the fact that dude was fine as hell with a little dick or the fact I didn't get that same friction and satisfaction I gave myself every day because I couldn't feel him inside of me!

Carl Thomas was a sexy, tall, brother that had a body God took his time sculpting, that is until he got to his penis. I honestly believe by the time God made his way to oh boy's penis he was tired and just tossed something there. I mean that's the only explanation I could come up with for that disappointment.

Then Carl had the audacity to walk around like he was the shit. I must admit I was convinced until we had sex, if that's what you want to call it. He wined and dined me for months before I decided to give it a go. Before I tell y'all what happened let me back up and explain something.

In the beginning I said I was a sexual being and couldn't wait to have sex. And that was true; still is. But as much as I wanted to be fucked, I wanted to be loved even more. So instead of fucking everything with a dick walking, I chose to wait for real love. Again, I experimented in other ways to get off, but I never allowed their dick to penetrate my pussy. I really thought I found love with Carl so when I finally felt we were at that stage in our relationship I didn't hesitate.

That night we had gone to dinner at a five-star restaurant then to a play on Broadway. The mood was so right. The night sky was clear. The stars twinkled brightly. The moon glowed to perfection. It wasn't too cold or too hot, but just right.

We kissed passionately as the cabbie drove us through the New York traffic. Our hands roamed and rubbed over each other. Carl placed his hand under my mini skirt and played with my clit, fingering my pussy just the way I like it. I immediately climaxed, moaning loudly. The damn cabbie almost had a wreck looking back at us.

By the time we made it to Carl's apartment, he had given me three orgasms by way of his fingers. As soon as we stepped inside his apartment, clothes came flying off and I was beyond ready to be fucked for the very first time.

He picked me up and carried me to his bedroom then gently laid me down on his bed. He knelt between my legs and ate my pussy as if I was a five-star meal. He licked every crevice, nibbled, and sucked on my clit, tonguing my second set of lips to my fourth orgasm. This was always the normal for us though. He'd put his finger in me just enough for me to feel him but not break my hymen.

I never actually saw his dick until that night. I touched him only through his pants, and what I felt seemed to be a pretty decent size. But I never felt him in my hands until that night. Before then I wondered why he didn't want me giving him blow jobs or jacking him off. The guys I dated prior to him and from what I heard from my best friends, Monica, and Tron; men liked that shit when they couldn't get the pussy.

Well we were finally about to get it on. But before we did, Carl cut the lights off before he took his boxers off. He climbed on top of me and started humping, grinding, and groaning. I'm lying there thinking what the fuck is he doing?! A couple minutes later and he was yelling out that he was coming. Hell, where did you go, I thought. This nigga had the nerve to roll over off me and onto the bed and go straight to sleep. Can someone tell me what the fuck went on, because surely, we did not have sex.

I was confused, disappointed, and pissed off all at the same time. I placed my hand under the sheet and felt for his dick. Seriously, I could not believe what I was not feeling. I turned the lamp on and removed the covers off Carl so I can see the truth. Low and behold, his dick was about the size of a thumb. And lying on the floor was a damn strap on. I put my

47

clothes on and left. There was no way in hell I could look homeboy in the face the next morning and tell him how great it was. It was garbage! And what man bamboozles a woman with a damn strap on? I'd felt better had he just used that instead of that little shit he really has. This was definitely a learning experience for me. Fuck that love shit! The next dude I get with, I'm going to make sure I see what he is working with up front because I can't put myself through that bullshit again.

Needless to say, I broke up with Carl. I didn't sugarcoat shit when I told him the reason. The funny thing about it though was that he took it very well. This led me to believe he has been hoodwinking women for a long time and is now used to being dumped.

It would be another year before I gave myself to another man and this time around, it was well worth the wait. I was doing my morning run through Central Park. It was now fall and the leaves were changing colors. The breeze was a bit chilly, but I was still sweating harshly due to my run. As I normally do while working out, I thought of my to-do list for the day at work as well as personal errands I needed to handle when a group of runners were coming towards me in a formation. As we passed, I got an eye full of the pact. They were all men and were from diverse backgrounds of ethnicities, variety of shades, different heights, and sizes. However, the one thing they had in common was how fine they were.

At first, I thought they may have been law enforcement or military, but that thought went out the window when this one brother came running by with diamond studs in both ears. He was the most beautiful man I'd ever laid my eyes on next to Carl. He was coco brown, with muscles for days. The gym shorts he wore clanged to a set of tone thighs that showcased a dick print looking more like a third leg. I instantly licked my lips at the sight. When our eyes met, staring back at me were a set of opal eyes that stared deep down into my soul. He looked familiar and I was wrecking my brain trying to figure out from where. He winked at me and I lost my footing, falling forward. I broke my fall on my hands before my face kissed the ground. Talk about an embarrassing moment!

"Are you alright?" A deep voice said from behind. A set of strong hands grabbed a hold of my waist. I turned around and was face to face with him.

For a what seemed like an eternity but was more so a few seconds, I got lost in space as my eyes roamed over his face. He looked like he was in his late twenties from a distance, but up close I saw that he was a bit older, maybe mid-thirties. His handsome face was blemish free. He had a small mole that sat just under his right nostril. His mustache and goatee were trimmed to perfection around his full lips. The smell of him had my pussy muscles contracting, ready to erupt like a volcano.

"Um, yes, I'm okay. I can be a bit of a klutz sometimes," I finally replied. He helped me up and I dusted myself off. "Thank you," I said smiling nervously at him. I looked around and was relieved when I saw no one around.

"You're welcome. And I'm going to need you to be careful. I can't have your clumsiness messing up your gorgeous face," Mr. Man said licking his lips.

I bit down on my bottom lip as my sweet nectar flowed onto my panties. If I was light-skinned my face would have been red from blushing.

"Don't do that," he said low enough so that only I could hear him.

I looked at him confused by what he was talking about until he said, "biting on your lip like that."

"Oh," was all I could say.

"I'm Romero, by the way. What's your name, beautiful?"

"Syntyche, but my friends call me Syn."

"A beautiful name for a beautiful woman. I like it. It's befitting." Romero said.

"Thanks." We just stood there eyeing each other, waiting for someone to make the next move.

I looked around again and didn't see any of his running group. By now they were probably on the other side of the park. We were all alone and anyone who was to pass us in that moment would have been able to feel as well as smell the sexual tension between us. It was just that thick in the air.

"Do you live near here?" Romero asked breaking the silence.

"I do. I'm just a few blocks from here. Are you asking because you want me to take you back to my place?" I asked getting right to it. There was no need for all the foreplay bullshit. I was horny and from his erect dick, he was too.

"Damn, beautiful and confident. I like that shit. And yes, I do. I would take you to mine but I don't live close by and I don't think I could go too much longer without tasting those sexy lips of yours."

"No need to wait," I said stepping up close to him. I pulled him down to my level by his shirt and planted my lips on his.

His soft lips parted, and our tongues snaked each other entwining with one another. He tasted of a peppermint as I sucked on his tongue, softly then harder. Romero grabbed my ass pulling me closer to him as our kiss deepened. I could feel his hardness against my pelvis, and it took everything within me not to strip right then.

"Damn, Rome, you weren't playing," a male voice said breaking our kiss. I wasn't sure how long we had been standing there kissing. I just know I was pissed off it was interrupted.

"Syntyche, this is my little brother Roderick. Rod this is Syn." Romero looked a bit embarrassed by his brother's statement.

"It's nice to meet you, Syn," Rod said holding out a hand for me to shake.

"Likewise. And what did you mean by him not playing?" I asked pointing to Romero.

"Oh well, uh Rome here saw you just as you came into the park, and uh he said he was going to get at you." Rod smiled deviously as he told me that. It didn't matter to me if Romero had an underlying reason because I really wanted to be fucked by him.

"Is that right?" I asked.

"It is," Romero quickly shot back. "To be quite honest, I've had my eyes on you for a while now."

I frowned at that statement because he was starting to sound like a stalker. He must have read my mind because he said, "No, I'm not stalking you. We've just been mingling in the same circles but each time I saw you, I couldn't get over to you to speak to you until now."

I looked him over again because I knew I too had seen him out somewhere, but it still wasn't coming to mind. This fine specimen could not be ignored. "Where have you seen me?"

I walked over to the bench and took a seat. Both men joined me. Rod hopped back up when he saw a slim, light skinned sister run passed us. I shook my head wondering how, why, would a woman pile a bunch of makeup on her face to go workout. If she really knew how thirsty she looked, she wouldn't do it. But what do I know? I guess Rod likes them dehydrated. I turned my attention back to Romero and waited for him to respond to my question.

"The first time I saw you was at a company function. You were with Carl Thomas. I must admit y'all looked good together and I felt some type of way about it." Romero sat back on the bench and stretched his long legs out. He placed an arm on the back of the bench and eyed me.

"You work with Carl?" I asked. I was wondering if Carl had mentioned to Romero that I broke up with him.

"No, I don't work with Carl. Carl works for me. I'm the CEO of Voltron Industry. Rod is my COO." Romero said matter of factly.

"You're Romero Bradford," I stated more so than asked. It was then I remembered him. Carl mentioned to me a couple of times who he worked for. I remember being at one of the parties and Carl pointed out Romero to

52

me. However, I thought it was the guy Romero was actually talking to as Carl's boss. Carl never corrected me either. And from how sexy he was, I saw why.

"Yes, I am. Is that a problem?" He asked me with concern.

"No. I'm just surprised is all. So, what has Carl told you about me? I'm sure you know we broke up since you haven't seen me at any of those functions anymore."

"I did ask about you, I think about six months ago. He was promoted to a managerial position. As always when we promote someone, we celebrate our employees with a party. When he showed up with another woman at his side, I had to ask what happened between the two of you." Romero chuckled.

"So, what did he say that got you laughing?"

"He said he broke up with you because you became too clingy and needy."

"What?!" I know that little dick bastard didn't say that shit.

"I'm laughing because just in this little time spent with you, I see he was lying."

"You damn right he was lying! The problem was his small dick."

"Whoa! Why you gonna put that man on front street like that?"

"Fuck him! He shouldn't have lied. Clingy and needy I am not nor will I ever be. He wasn't equipped to handle all this," I said running my hands down the side of my curvy body.

"But you were with him for almost a year. So, now you're saying he has a little dick?" Romero asked in disbelief.

"We were together eight months and we didn't have sex but one time. That one time was the first and last time because I broke up with him. And that was on our eight-month anniversary," I explained.

"Are you serious?"

"Very much so."

"Why? Y'all were two consenting adults. Why did it take so long? If you don't mind me asking.?"

"I was a virgin. Hell, I believe I'm still one, because I didn't feel anything when he was supposed to have been inside me," I admitted with a shrug.

"Wait, wait, wait. Hold up. So, you're telling me you're a virgin?" Romero looked stunned.

"Yes. Technically I am being my hymen is still intact. During our time together, Carl and I got off in other ways. He ate my pussy, fingered me, and all that but we never had real sex."

I placed my head in the palms of my hands because I couldn't believe I was sitting there telling a total stranger about my damn sex life. What is wrong with me? I stood up preparing to leave. "I have to go. I got to get ready for work."

"Hey, don't feel embarrassed by all this. I'm not judging at all. It's actually refreshing to hold a conversation with a woman who is authentic,"

Romero hooked a finger under my chin and lifted my head up to look at him.

"That's what you're saying, but what are you really thinking?"

"I'm thinking I want to spend more time with you. I want to get to know you more. I can't deny that I want to get you in bed, but I'm not going to rush you on that."

"Why not? Before this conversation you were trying to go home with me."

"I was and I still do. But I see I found a rare gem. I have to handle you with care."

"Being a virgin or something else?"

"Both actually. As I said earlier, I've had my eyes on you for a while. Now that I know you're available, I'm shooting my shot. Trust I'm going to hit the bullseye."

I nodded my head. "We shall see, but don't you mean make the basket, as in basketball?" I laughed at his metaphor.

"Yeah, well either way, I'm trying to get at you. So, can I take you to dinner tonight?" Romero asked. He looked passed me and I turned to see what he was looking at. We watched Rod walking back towards us with the chic he went after a few minutes ago.

"What time and what's the dress code?" I asked turning back to face Romero. He frowned at his brother once he and the woman were standing next to us.

"Rome, Syn, this is Devon." Rod said.

"Hi! It's so wonderful to meet you, Romero. I've heard so much about you!" Devon exaggerated. It was clear she knew who he was and was trying to shoot her shot. This bitch didn't even acknowledge me.

"Bruh, really?" Romero asked ignoring Devon.

"What?" Rod asked dumbfounded.

"You sure know how to pick them," Romero shook his head.

"I work for Preston and Garrison PR Firm. If you ever need my services, you can call me anytime," she said pulling out a business card from her pants pocket. I snatched it out of her hand and handed it to Rod.

" Nah, sus, he won't be needing that card or any of your services," I ain't the jealous type so that's not what pissed me off. It was her blatant disrespect towards everyone standing there. And if she said the wrong thing, I was gonna shove that damn business card down her throat.

"That was rude," Devon pouted.

"Nah what was rude was you bopping your ass over here, flirting with me when you are with my brother. Then you rudely ignore this woman standing next to you," Romero said. He grabbed my hand then looked at Rod and said, "Don't bring her anywhere near me or my business or we will have some problems, bro. Come on."

We left the couple standing there as we made our way out of the park. Romero held on to my hand as we approached a black Infiniti SUV. One of the guys in the running group stood next to the vehicle. "Can I give you a ride?" Romero asked.

"No thanks. I'm going to run the few blocks back to my building."

"Okay, so tonight I want to have you all to myself, just you and me. So, I'm going to cook your dinner at my place. You can dress as casually as you'd like. Can I see your cell phone?"

I pulled my phone out and handed it to him after I unlocked it. He typed in his number and a few seconds later, his cell phone began ringing. He ended the call then handed me back my phone.

"Now we have each other's number. Text me your address and I'll have Mario here pick you up, say around eight."

"Yes, eight sounds good."

"Cool. Until then, have a good day." Romero leaned down and kissed me on the lips. At first it was a short peck, but it turned into a war of tongues as we got lost in that kiss. We forgot all about where we were until Mario cleared his throat.

"Sir, you must go. Now," Mario said, tilting his head to his right.

Some paparazzi were snapping away with their cameras. Surely, they got that kiss on film. They began shouting out questions asking about me and if I was his flavor of the month. Flashes from the camera blinded me as they got closer to us.

"Shit! I'm sorry, Syn, but I must insist I take you home," Romero said agitated and sorrowful.

I couldn't turn down his offer now and quickly slid in the back seat of the SUV. Romero followed behind and Mario immediately closed the door. He ran around to the driver side, shoving the paparazzi to the side so that he could get in. As soon as he was seated behind the wheel, I rattled off my address to him. He slowly pulled off into traffic, careful not to hit any of the reporters or another vehicle.

This was something I had never experienced before so I was a little scared. I was trembling all over as if the winter weather had swooped in. Romero wrapped an arm around me, trying to comfort me. But it was clear he was upset by the situation. "I bet that bitch made the call," he said with disdain.

He pulled his phone out and made a call. "Rodrick, did that woman alert the paparazzi I was at that park?" He listened to whatever Rod was saying on the other end of the line.

"Bruh, that broad is an opportunist. Didn't you catch that shit seeing her with all that damn makeup piled on her damn face, yet she is working out in the park?"

I laughed at that comment. Seeing that we were pulling up in front of my building, I tapped him on his leg. "I'll see you tonight," I mouthed to him.

"I'll get at you at the office," Romero said and hung up. Turning to me he said, "I'm gonna need some lip locking before you go, though," he eyed me intently and I found myself turned on.

"Come walk me to my door," I said seductively.

"You don't have to tell me twice," Romero said and followed me as I exited the door Mario held opened. "I'll call you when I'm ready," he told Mario.

"Yes, sir," Mario nodded then looked and me. He smiled and said, "Good day, Ma'am."

"Thanks. Same to you," I told him

Fred, the door attendant, held open the door to the lobby of my building, nodding to us as we entered. I led Romero to the elevator. It opened as soon as we approached. Mrs. Gable, my neighbor across from me, exited with her dog, Fluffy, in tow. She tried to hold a conversation, but I quickly shut her down, pulling Romero inside the elevator. I pressed the button to the twelfth floor. As soon as the doors closed, Romero pulled me in and smashed his lips against mine. We kissed the entire ride up to my floor.

The ding announcing it made it to my floor is what broke our kiss. We made our way to my apartment. Romero stood so close to me as I placed my key in the lock, his hard dick pressed against my ass. He gave it a slap just as I opened the door.

"You can get the grand tour another time," I told Romero as I led him down the hall to my bedroom.

I went inside my walk-in closet and footed off my sneakers. When I turned around, I gasped at the site before me. Romero stood at the closet entrance wearing nothing but his skin. His dick pointed out at me as if it was beckoning me to him. "My damn."

59

"I showed you mine. Now show me yours," Romero joked.

"With pleasure," I began a strip tease, slowly pulling my tank top over my head. I turned my back then pulled my sports bra over my head. I tossed over my shoulder at him. In a seductive manner, I pulled my leggings down along with my panties, bending over so he could get a good look at all my glory. Once I stepped out of my leggings and panties, I turned to face Romero.

"Beautiful," Romero said. "Bring your fine ass over here."

I sauntered over to him, trying to hold my nervousness in. Romero's dick was huge, way bigger than Carl's little dick. Shit I can't lie; I was scared he was gonna rip me a new pussy and asshole looking at the size of him. He must have picked up on my nervousness because he took a step back once I was within arm's reach of him. I was taken aback by his movement and all of a sudden, I felt dirty. I wrapped my arms around my waist feeling insecure.

"No, baby, don't think I'm rejecting you. I can see you're scared and the last thing I want to do is pressure you into anything. If you're not ready, you're not ready. And I totally respect that." Romero looked sincere.

"I am nervous, but I am ready, Romero. I've been in a number of relationships and could have given myself to any of those guys, but I didn't. I really loved Carl and thought he was the one. But I knew I was not going to be satisfied with our sex life if I remained in in that relationship and eventually, I would step out on him. That's real talk. But you, you look at me and I'm wet and ready," I admitted.

"Why?"

"Why what?" I asked confused.

"Why are you wet and ready for me?" Romero asked with all seriousness.

I walked over to my bed and plopped down on it. "Honestly, I don't know. I just know there is definitely something between us. This is truly the first time I've been this freakin' open with a man. I have never thrown myself at a man the way I've done with you."

Trust me when I say, this is something new happening with me. I mean, I've always been straight forward, but when it came to men, I was never this aggressive. I guess it was because I was feeling something for this man that I've never felt before. Whatever the case, I knew I wanted him in every possible way.

"What do you feel towards me?" Romero asked, taking a seat on the bed next to me. He grabbed my hand and held onto it.

I know, I know. You're reading this thinking, that has to be some weird shit with those two sitting there butt ass naked talking about their feelings instead of getting it on. Trust me, it was weird, but I'm glad we did, because had we not done that then the following actions may not have taken place.

"Well, I have butterflies in my stomach right now. Not in a bad way, but a good way. I want you in every way possible. I want to get to know you and spend time with you as well. But right now, I really want you inside of me. I want to feel you in me," I climbed further onto the bed, pulling him with me.

"Don't you want to know how I feel?" Romero asked climbing on top of me.

"I do, but I'm okay with you telling me afterwards. I'm tired of talking. So, shut up and fuck me already."

"Say no more," Romero replied.

He pulled a nipple into his mouth, suckling on it as he rubbed the other nipple between his fingers. He then took the other nipple in his mouth and repeated the process. He moved down to my recently waxed love box and pulled my clit into his mouth. He rolled his tongue around my clit and between my folds. He inserted two of his fingers inside me and moved them in and out. I gyrated my pussy on his fingers and tongue, sparks shooting from my pussy down my legs. "Oh god!" I screamed.

I can't even describe to y'all the feeling that was taking over my body as Romero ate my pussy! Y'all, this man had me ready to put a ring on his finger! Whew, chile! As my orgasm started, I saw flashes of light, my body began to shake uncontrollably, and my breathing quickened. "Oh shit! Ooh shit! Ro-mer-ooooo!" My orgasm shot through from between my legs then rushed up to my brain and back down to my toes. Lawd, I have never, and I do mean never experienced an orgasm as intense as that.

"Damn, you taste so good," Romero said as he continued to lap up my juices that was still pouring out of me.

When he finally came up, I couldn't help but laugh at how my nectar had him looking like a glazed donut. I have never been a squirter, or at least no one has ever been able to take me there, but on that day, Romero made a believer out of me. My juices splashed all over his face was proof in the pudding. I grabbed some tissue from the nightstand and wiped his face off. I intentionally missed his lips since I wanted to taste myself on them.

I spread my legs wider opening myself up completely to Romero. He placed the head of his massive sausage at my opening. He slid only the tip in and out. My walls were so tight I didn't think he would fit. He slid in further hitting my hymen. I tensed up feeling him breaking his way in. "Relax, baby. It'll be a bit painful, but once you get passed the pain, you're going to feel so much pleasure." Romero said.

He leaned down and began kissing me as inched further inside me. Then he bit down on my neck as he broke my hymen and entered me fully. "Aaaahhh!" I screamed out. That shit hurt like hell! "Wait, don't move," I told him. I had to get acclimated with him inside me. Once the stinging stopped. I nodded my head for Romero to move.

He slowly slid back and forth inside my pussy. He was right. I began to feel the pleasure of him, and boy did he feel good. I started imitating his strokes, matching his moves. We quickly picked up the pace and I threw my pussy as if I had been fucking for decades. Romero filled me completely and it started to feel like his dick had reached the center of my stomach. He was just that long.

"Syn, baby, you feel so good." Romero placed a leg in the crook of his arm and started pounding into me. "Oh shit! This pussy belongs to me now."

"Oh, oh, oh, aaahh," was all I could say. This man had me feeling as if I was high on ecstasy.

Romero hit my spot and I yelled out in pleasure so loud, I know my neighbors heard me. "Mmm hmm, I found that g-spot," he crooned in my ear.

He kept hitting my spot with precision. My pussy rewarded him by contracting fast and hard around his dick, pulsating as my orgasm grew. I felt like my soul had come out of me as I gushed with pleasure. My eyes rolled to the back of my head as I released everything in me. I dug my nails into Romero's back holding on for dear life. Romero continued to stroke inside of me, removing the leg that was in his arm and replacing it with the other leg. He fucked me so good, I swear I saw God himself at the Pearly Gates!

"Shit, Syn, I'm about to cum, baby!" Romero said. I could feel the tip of his dick swell from the nut he was about to burst, and before I could say something, Romero shot his load inside of me. He nutted so hard and long, it felt like he released a whole damn river of semen in me. "Oh, shit!" Romero shouted. He shook until he was completely empty, then collapsed on top of me.

As we lay there trying to catch our breath, I couldn't help but to notice how I could still feel Romero inside of me even after he'd nutted. Damn, his dick is just that thick! And my pussy was still contracting around him. When he moved to get off me, I had a mini orgasm as he pulled out of me. Wow!

"Are you alright?" Romero asked me once his breathing was back to normal. He turned on his side then pulled me closer to him.

"I'm good. No, I'm better than good. I'm great!" I said turning on my side so that we were facing each other.

He pulled my leg over his then rested his arm around my waist. We lay there holding each other and staring into each other's eyes. All of a sudden, I burst out laughing at the giddy feeling floating around in my belly. I rolled my eyes thinking how crazy I must have been looking to Romero. As I said earlier, I've had my share of relationships, and they were with some of the finest, educated, and wealthiest men in the state of New York. However, I've never felt this feeling towards them that I'm feeling for Romero. My feelings for Carl don't even come close, and I know I was in love with him. Or at least, I think I was.

"What's so funny?" Romero broke my thoughts.

"This feeling I'm having in the pit of my belly again. I don't know what this means."

"Mmm," Romero hummed. "So, you feeling a brother, huh?"

"Maybe," I teased.

"Maybe?"

"Okay, sort of," I continued to taunt him.

"Woman, I see you got jokes," Romero said as he started tickling me.

"Aahh! Okay, okay. I am! I am!" I shouted between laughter.

"That's more like it," Romero said rolling over onto me.

My legs voluntarily opened for him, welcoming all he had to offer. He slid in me with ease and we were back at it again. I lifted my head to kiss him. Our tongues played a game of tug and war as our bodies moved in unison. My nails raked across his back as he nibbled on my ear lobe. I spread my legs as far as they would allow and pulled him in deeper. Romero felt oh so good inside of me. I swear he fit like a glove, like his dick was molded to perfectly fit inside my pussy. Or maybe it was because Romero was the only man to ever enter my love canal.

"I want to ride," I told Romero. I was feeling a bit cocky and wanted to ride him the same way I saw a chic doing in a porno flick I watched a while back. He looked surprised by my comment but didn't protest. He pulled out and laid on his back. He placed his hands behind his head and waited for me to do my thing.

Before I climbed on top, I decided I wanted to show him my oral skills. I positioned myself between his legs on my knees. I bent down and wrapped my mouth around the head, sucking on it, tasting the mixture of our fluids. I sucked him further in my mouth until I had every inch down my throat. I massaged his balls while contracting my throat the same way I do with my pussy walls. This always drove men wild, and now Romero was added to the list.

"Ooh shit! Goddamn, Syn!" Romero belted out. I smiled because that was always the reaction I got, that was until I hummed. "Fuck! Shit! Oh shit!" Romero shouted. Yep! That's what they all said! Tehehe!

I eased him out of my mouth with a pop. I sat up and smiled at my handy work. Romero lay sprawled out on the bed with a look of pure bliss plastered on his face. I crawled up and positioned the head at my opening and slid down on him. We both moaned as I was filled completely. Playing the porno in my mind, I began rolling my hips in a clockwise motion, bouncing up and down in the process. Shit this felt so good! I'm in love with dick riding! I gyrated and grinded my hips on Romero. I turned and rode him on the side continuing to bounce up and down. I kept turning on his dick until I was riding him cowgirl style.

Placing my hands behind me to steady my balance, I bounced up and down, squeezing my walls as I came up and releasing as I slid down. Then I rotated my hips in a circular motion giving his dick a feel of my walls from every angle. I turned again so that I was riding him from the side, then turning so that I was back facing him.

"Syn, shit, baby! Ride this dick," Romero grunted in pleasure. He grabbed a hold of my ass and pumped up in me. I could tell he was on the verge of coming but didn't want to because he took control of how fast I bounced up and down on him. That was fine by me because my orgasm began building up. My legs began shaking uncontrollably just as my walls began contracting. I let Romero do the work from the bottom as I climaxed, my juices gushing down Romero's dick and squirting out all around us.

"Oh, Romero!" I rode that wave like a surfer. And a couple pumps more, he held tightly to my waist and shot his nut up in me. He fell back onto the bed pulling me down on him. He held me close to his chest and we fell asleep that way.

The ringing of my cell phone woke me up. I'm not sure how long I was asleep. My body felt worn out but tingled from the pleasures it had endured. The ringing stopped then started back up. I rolled over to answer it and it was then I realized I was alone in my bed. There was no sign of Romero as if I had dreamed the lovemaking session. But the way my body was tingling I knew it really did happen.

The phone started back ringing. I quickly grabbed and answered without checking the caller ID. "Hello."

"You better have a foot in your grave or be laid up in the hospital," my supervisor, Lisa gritted through the line.

"Lisa, I'm sorry I didn't call you earlier. But I really am not feeling well," I lied. Looking at the clock, it read five fifteen. Damn, my ass was knocked out!

"Syntyche, we had to reschedule the meeting you called about the Diplo campaign. That's not how I get down and you know it." Lisa was pissed, needless to say.

I'm the VP of marketing for the Manchurian Advertising Firm. We, or shall I say, I went hard to bring Michael and Dominque Diplo on board as clients. Today was supposed to be my grand pitch for their new skin care line that's about to hit the market. They are the powerhouse couple that behind Diplo Cosmetics. I literally bumped into Dominque on the street one day and that led to a meeting that led to them signing with us. I had been working around the clock putting this ad campaign together and just like that I fucked it up by fucking. Ain't that a bitch?

"Lisa, you know how hard I worked on this campaign. And you know I'm always the first one in the door and the last to leave, so cut me some slack, please. I'll be in tomorrow."

"You better and since you made this mess, you better fix it!" Lisa hung up without another word.

I laid back on the bed and gathered my thoughts. I thought over the events that took place this morning and was astound they happened to me. Shaking my head, I climbed out of bed and went into my bathroom. I ran some bath water, adding aromatherapy bath oil. I sat on the toilet and relieved myself. Once I was done, I moved to the sink and washed my hands. I went back into my bedroom and grabbed my cell phone. I checked for a missed call or an unread text from Romero, but there was none. Before jumping to conclusions, I called him, but I got sent to his voicemail.

"Hey, it's me, Syntyche. I was just giving you a call since you left without waking me. Give me a call back when you get this message," I hung up, then said aloud to no one in particular, "Damn, I believe I got played."

I went back into the bathroom and cut the water off. Easing down in the water, my body relaxed but my mind was all over the place. Did I really get played by him? Carl didn't tell him I was clingy and needy. He knew before I told him what really happened between Carl and me. As much as I want to be mad, I can't. Shit, if I was to be mad, I'd have to be mad at myself. I practically served my cookie to him on a platter. Well, I can honestly say it was well worth it.

Letting thoughts of him leave my mind, I washed my body then got out the tub. I applied body oil to my body then dressed in a pair of boy shorts and a tank top. I went to the kitchen, started a pot of coffee, then looked through the fridge for something quick to fix. I grabbed the shrimp I thawed and seasoned to cook last night, but didn't, along with the onion, garlic, pepper, butter, and box of grits. Setting the ingredients on the counter, I pulled out a pot and ran some water in it before placing it on top of the stove. I pulled out a pan and placed it on the stove also.

I turned on Sirius XM radio to the Heart & Soul channel. Beyoncé's Dance for You blared through the speakers. I danced around the kitchen as I prepared my shrimp and grits. I fixed my plate and was about to dig in when my cell phone beeped with a text message. I looked at the screen and saw it was a message from Monica. I unlocked my phone and read her message.

Monica: Bih, wyd

Me: eating, wassup

Monica: y ur ass wasn't @ work 2day

Me: long story u wouldn't believe

My phone began ringing. I answered already knowing it was Monica calling to be nosey. "What do you want, heifer?" I joked.

"Bitch, I'm calling to get the tea. Why were you MIA from work today? And tell me everything. Don't leave nothing out," she demanded.

"Yeah, bitch, spill the tea," my other best friend, Tron said.

"Damn, that's how y'all gonna do me?"

"Yep," they said in unison.

"Well," I began telling them everything that went down today from meeting Romero to Lisa calling and giving me the business. There was complete silence on the other end when I was done. "Hello, is anyone there?" I asked.

"Damn, Syn, for once you let your freak flag fly!" Tron said with excitement. "Like, Sis, you gave yourself to a complete stranger today. Then the muthafucka left your ass laid the fuck out!"

"Seriously, Syn, make sure you schedule an appointment with your doctor to get checked for STDs. You let that nigga go in raw. Ain't no telling if he clean or not," Monica said. For once, she was the voice of reason.

"I know to all of that. I got caught up. But y'all, I really feel something for him. I ain't never felt this way about a man before. I just hate I got played. And the fucked-up thing is I don't want to fuck with anyone else. I swear, y'all, his dick was made for me."

"Syntyche, please get your head out of the clouds. He was your first, so yes you think that. But trust me, Sis, now that you've gotten your cherry officially popped, you'll find some new dick, bigger and better than what homeboy dished out," Monica said.

"I'm with Mo on this, baby girl, you got to move on from this," Tron chimed.

"I hear ya," I solemnly said.

"You hear us, but are you listening?" Monic asked.

"Yes—" I started but was cut off from the buzzing of my doorbell. "Hold on, y'all. Somebody's at my door."

I listened to my best friends chatting as I went to the door and looked through the peephole. To my surprise, it was him. Romero was at my door. My breath got caught in my throat. I didn't think I'd be seeing him anymore. He knocked causing me to jump back. Gathering myself, I opened the door and stood face to face with him.

"Hi," Romero said.

"Hi," I replied.

"Syn, who is at your door?" Tron asked in my ear.

"I'll call y'all back," I told them and hung up before they could rattle off any more questions.

Romero and I stood at the door looking at each other, no one saying anything, just staring. He was dressed in a charcoal grey suit, with a white shirt and tie matching the suit. His loafers were buffed to a high shine. He looked like a man of power in that suit, fine as hell.

"Are you going to let me in, or are we going to stand here looking each other over all night?" Romero asked.

"Y-yeah, come in," I stood to the side allowing him to pass. He kissed me lightly on the lips once he was in front of me. I closed the door, locked it, then ushered him to the kitchen where I was sitting.

"Would you like something to drink?"

"What do you have? Do you have any leftovers from your dinner? A brother can eat right about now." Romero took his suit jacket off and hung it behind the chair. He loosened his tie and unbuttoned the top button of his shirt and his cuffs.

"I have water, milk, beer, wine, brown, and white liquor."

"I'll take a shot of whatever brown you have along with a beer, please."

"Coming up. I made shrimp and grits. Are you cool with that?"

"Yes, ma'am."

I moved about the kitchen fixing his drink and food. I handed him everything then took a seat across from him. I watched him as he tossed the shot of Crown Royal then followed that with the beer. He said a prayer then dug into the shrimp and grits. He closed his eyes while he chewed on his food.

"Mmm, this is so good. Let me find out you can cook," Romero said after swallowing.

"Hey, what can I say? I got skills," I chuckled.

"Indeed," he replied.

"So why did you leave and not say anything today?" I asked. I needed to hear his reasoning behind all this.

"You were sleeping so peaceful. I just didn't want to disturb you."

"Okay why didn't you answer my call or my text earlier?"

"I was in meetings all day and I don't take my phone in any meetings to avoid being distracted. I figured showing up in person would be better than calling or texting you back. So here I am," Romero explained.

I took in everything he had to say, watching him, and listening intently, looking for any signs of a lie. I couldn't find one. He was telling the truth. This made me smile. I stood and walked over to him. I sat on his lap and wrapped my arms around his neck. I kissed him tenderly then took the spoon from him and began feeding him. He slipped a hand under my tank top and grabbed a breast. He gave it a squeeze then began playing with my nipple. It hardened to his touch and a moan escaped me. My doorbell buzzed interrupting our bit of foreplay.

"Are you expecting company?"

"Nah, but I know it ain't nobody but one or both of my besties," I said rising from Romero's lap and making my way to the door. Sure enough, both Monica and Tron stood there with fake ass concerned looks on their faces.

"We came to check on you, best friend," Mo said shoving me to the side as she entered. Tron followed behind her.

I shook my head at those two. I closed the door then made my way back to the kitchen. Romero was at the sink running dish water, while my friends moved around the kitchen like they were at home. I walked over to Romero so I could make the introductions. "Romero, these are my two best friends, Monica and Tron. Mo, Tron, this is Romero."

"Hey," Mo and Tron sang in unison.

"Hey," Romero said then held out his hand for them to shake.

"You know, we had written you off," Tron stated.

"Oh?" Romero asked with an eyebrow raised. He looked over at me for confirmation. I turned to the sink and began washing the dishes. I wanted no parts of that conversation. If he is going to be a part of my life, he's going to have to be able to deal with my friends.

"I thought you were running some type of game on my sista," Monica admitted.

"Well, I assure you, you, and you, Syntyche, I am not. I don't play those types of games. I'm feeling your girl. Have been for quite some time now. And after today, I'm not going anywhere," Romero said.

"I'll take that," Tron replied. "Syn is good peoples and I don't want her to get hurt. She put herself out there for you today in ways I've never known her to do in the lifetime I've known her. So yeah, we were feeling some type of way about how you left her today."

"I'm glad Syn has great friends like the two of you, but I'm not here to hurt her. She is it for me, was the first time I laid eyes on her." Romero walked over and stood behind me. He wrapped his arms around my waist. "So, you don't have to worry about me going anywhere," he crooned in my ear. He tilted my head back and kissed me.

"Awwee," Tron and Monica cooed.

"Well, since we know you are good, sis, we out," Tron said standing. He grabbed Monica by the arm pulling her to her feet.

"Fool let me go," Monica fussed. She came over and gave me a hug then waved bye to Romero. Tron followed behind. I walked them to the door and promised to meet them for happy hour Friday night.

I went back to the kitchen to find Romero cleaning up what was left in the kitchen. "You don't have to do that. I can finish it."

"I don't mind," he said wiping down the countertop.

I leaned against the wall and watched in awe as Romero cleaned my kitchen. I'm sure he had a whole staff of people to do that for him at his place. Whatever the case, I was turned on by it. With his back to me sweeping the floor, I stripped out of my clothes then leaned back against the wall. He stopped in his tracks when he saw me standing there naked. I could see the tent in his pants as his dick got hard. I smiled then left him in the kitchen. I made my way to the bedroom. I stripped down the sheets from earlier and replaced them with some clean ones.

"You full of sass, Ms. Syntyche," Romero entered the room stroking his massive cock.

"I am. What are you going to do about it?" I asked crawling to the center of the bed.

"I think I'm going to have to smack that ass," he answered walking over to me.

"Ooh, I just might like that," I turned with my back to him. On all fours, I tooted my ass up toward his face, arching my back. I twerked my ass like a stripper on a pole. Romero smacked me on my left cheek then my right. "Umm," I moaned.

Romero rubbed the head of his dick up and down the slit of my opening. Then he tapped it against my clit. I could feel my juices streaming out and onto the head I was so wet. "Put it in," I demanded. "Aaah," I moaned as Romero plummeted in me.

Romero stroked me hard and fast, his balls slapping against me. I met his strokes popping my pussy on his dick to the rhythm we made. I pushed my ass further into him wanting him to reach my bottom. He leaned down and placed a hand on my clit. "Oh, yes. Just like that," I moaned.

"You like this?" Romero asked. He slapped me on my ass. I moaned again. "Answer me. You like this?" He asked again.

"Yeessss," I moaned. "Mmm, Rome! Oh yes!"

"Sssss, mmm," Romero hissed. "Say my name again like that," he pumped faster, harder. He found my g-spot and knocked the head against it. He continued to circle my clit with his finger.

"Aah, Ro-ome! R-rome! Damn, I'm about to come!" Before I could get that statement out fully, I started skeeting. It felt like I was peeing and couldn't hold it. I kept gushing with each stroke. Romero didn't let up either. He kept hitting my g-spot bringing on another high-intense orgasm. It had me so weak I fell forward onto the bed. Romero followed and had me like Tommy had ole girl in Belly. He rode me through my second and third orgasm before he nutted inside me.

"Syn, Syn, Syn." Romero said my name over and over as we laid out on the bed.

"Rome, Rome, Rome," I mimicked.

He moved off me and over on the side of me. He slapped me on my ass playfully. I jiggled it and we both laughed. "Come, let's shower. And if you don't mind, would you come with me to my place tonight?"

"Ah, I have to work tomorrow. I definitely have to be there and on time tomorrow. I missed an important meeting today because you knocked me out."

"I'm sorry. Please accept my apologies. I hope I didn't get you into any trouble."

"No worries. I just need to be there tomorrow, though," I said climbing out of bed.

We christened the shower, twice, then washed each other. I put on a pair of leggings and t-shirt. I packed an overnight bag and made sure I had all my files for my meeting tomorrow. My legs felt like jello when I tried to stand up and felled back onto the bed. I couldn't help but laugh at the situation.

"What's so funny?" Romero asked walking into the bedroom.

"My legs are noodles. I can't stand. You literally wore my ass out today," I laughed.

"Come on, baby, I got ya. Hop on." Romero bent down in front of me so I could climb on his back.

"You have got to be kidding, right?"

"Nah, hop on. I'll carry you. You're in good hands," Romero said.

"This is so embarrassing," I giggled as I climbed onto his back. I wrapped my arms around his neck and once he stood, he hooked his arms under my legs as I wrapped them around his waist. He carried me through the house making sure everything was turned off before I set the alarm and we left out.

Mrs. Gable came walking down the hall with Fluffy and I waved at her as we passed by. She stood to the side looking stunned at us. I giggled as Romero galloped down the hall to the elevators. He pressed the down button and it opened. He stepped on a pressed the L button for the lobby. I watched our reflection through the professionally polished elevator and could see how much we complimented each other. I could see his genuineness as he smiled at me. I smiled back. It was right then that I knew I would spend the rest of my life with Romero Bradford.

"You're stuck with me, Syntyche Moore. I just want you to know that," Romero said.

"Likewise, Romero Bradford. Likewise."

I know y'all thinking there ain't no way this bitch met a rich, good looking man, fucked him that same day, and got her happily ever after! Well guess what? Yes, this bitch did. We were married five months later with only our closest family and friends attending the ceremony. And nine months to the day we met, and I lost my virginity, I gave birth to our first child, Sarai Rosemary Bradford. I kept with my mom and grandma's tradition by giving our child a name from the bible.

Romero and I have been happily married for ten years now. We had two more children, Romero, Jr., and Jacob. We've had our ups and downs, but the love has never dwindled. That flame is still lit and as long as I have breath in my body, Romero Carron Bradford will always be my one and only.

Chapter 5: A Stormy Night

Cooper and I decided to stay in instead of going out because it was storming something serious outside. I made us deli sandwiches, placed some chips in a bowel, and grabbed the bottle of wine I had chilling to make up a picnic on our bedroom floor. Cooper, on the other hand, had a different idea.

"Come here," he says laying in the bed butt ass naked.

My mouth and pussy watered at the sight of my man's chiseled body spread eagle awaiting me. I could have sworn Mr. Big, his dick, winked at me. I placed the contents I had in my hand on the dresser and then began to do a sexy strip tease for Cooper before climbing into bed once I was nude. I crawled up to his throbbing dick and licked the head. "Umm, so good," I whimpered before deep throating all ten inches. Cooper moaned as I began to suck his dick. I bobbed up and down slurping his precum in the process.

"Damn, baby," he said as I massaged his balls. He slightly tugged my hair, which was his way of telling me he was ready to be inside my second set of lips.

I eased him out of my mouth and kissed the tip. I climbed on top of Cooper and positioned the head at the entry of my honey pot. I slid down and rested a second allowing my walls to adjust to Mr. Big before I began rotating my hips. Just as I found my rhythm, Cooper flipped me over and rammed his massive dick in me. "Aahh!" I yelled out from the pleasure and pain.

"Back that ass up on it," Cooper barked and smacked me on my right ass cheek. I obeyed and arched my back. Cooper grabbed a handful of my hair and smacked my ass again. "Yes, just like that," he moaned.

I screeched while tightening my pussy muscles around his dick. Cooper stroked and stroked hitting every angle. "Oh, yeah! Take this dick!" he yelled as he pulled my hair a bit harder.

"Mmm, shit!" Cooper found my spot and began to murder it. His thrusts were so long and deep that my moans got caught in my throat as I began to come.

"Uumm hhmmm! That's what it's made for!" Cooper cried out as he felt my orgasm take over and my juices rained down. He pumped harder as he felt his nut getting ready to burst. "Shit, Robin," he called out my name as he released inside me. Cooper collapsed on top of me and we fell asleep that way.

The sound of the rain as well as the cool breeze that blew in from the crack of the window stirred me out of my slumber. I smiled to myself as memories of last night flashed across my mind. I smiled wider because our bodies are still intertwined with each other. I can feel "Mr. Big" at my opening, impatiently waiting to enter me.

"Good morning, sweetheart," my lover said to me before planting a kiss between my shoulder blades. I arched my back and he entered me with one thrust. "I see someone is ready for round two," he whispered in my ear and stroked deeper.

"Oohh," I moaned and tooted my ass up to take in further all that "Mr. Big" had to offer me. The sounds of our bodies smacking against one another as well as our moans filled our bedroom as we made love passionately. "Oh baby, I'm about to come!" I screamed as my legs began to tremble from the massive orgasm that was taking over me.

"Say my name!" he demanded as he picked up the pace.

"Cooper!" I yelled and came so hard I almost lost consciousness. A couple of strokes later and Cooper exploded, releasing his seed inside of me. He then rolled over onto his back trying to catch his breath. We both lay quietly until our breathing was back to normal.

"Damn, babe, you gonna have me walking around in the daylight with a flashlight looking for you!" Cooper joked. I laughed at him and planted a kiss on his lips as I jumped out of bed and headed towards our master bathroom.

"Come shower with me and we can go another round before I have to get ready for work."

"Say no more, ma!" Cooper hopped out of bed to come join me, smacking me on my ass upon entering the shower.

The bathroom steamed up from the heat of the water as it pounded down upon us. Cooper poured some of the shea butter body wash onto a loofa and began washing my body. My kitty purred as he swiped the loofah across my nipple and around each breast, one at a time. He continued to wash my body down my belly and between my legs. He lingered there gently rubbing the loofah between the folds of my pussy lips. Each stroke of the soft fabric across my kitty sent sparks throughout my body. Not able to withstand our bodies being connected, I turned to face my man, put a foot up on the wall behind him and spread my pussy open with my fingers. "Put him in," I demanded.

Cooper tossed the loofah in the tray then positioned the tip of Mr. Big at my opening. So eager to have him inside me, I arched my back off the shower wall, grabbed Cooper by the waist and pulled him into me causing his dick to slide inside my pussy. I gasped at the feel of him inside of me. My pussy walls contracted as he invaded my love nest.

The feel of the water pounding down on me as Cooper pumped in and out of my pussy had my body on fire. Each stroke Cooper made felt like a match being struck against the box trying to be ignited. And the water cascading down was fuel to the fire that blazed our love making throughout the bathroom. With one hand Cooper grabbed ahold of an ass cheek and went deeper inside my tunnel. With the other hand he slid a finger inside my asshole and stroked in and out driving me wild.

My leg became week as my orgasm began taking over. Cooper then picked me up and pumped faster and harder bringing my orgasm to its peak the way only he knew how to do it. I threw my head back holding on with my arms wrapped around his neck and enjoyed the ride as I climaxed so long my teeth chattered, and my body twitched.

"You might as well call your assistant and tell her you will be working from home because I'm not letting up out of this pussy for a while," Cooper said as he continued to stroke my sweet spot.

I couldn't utter any words, so I shook my head to let him know I was in agreeance with him. Oh, how I loved my husband and what he did to me. He knew exactly what I needed and when, which was I didn't put up a fuss about his statement. There was no way I could go the remainder of the day after being fucked royally this way. He knew when we got down like this, it would take a whole day of him dicking me down until I begged for mercy before I couldn't go on.

He pulled out and placed me on my feet. I kneeled down and took him into my mouth, slurping my juices mixed with the water down my throat. I knew he needed my oral action in that moment. He was on the verge of coming and wasn't quite ready. Because he only cums in my pussy, I sucked him long enough to get him harder. I stood back up and bend over in front of him. I felt his tongue run down my asshole. I moaned at the pleasurable feel of his tongue darting in and out of my asshole while he fingered my pussy.

The water was beginning to get cold but that didn't stop us from continuing our fuck fest. I grinded my pelvis on his finger and tongue as another orgasm came on bringing me to ecstasy. My legs quivered underneath me, and Cooper had to wrap an arm around my waist to hold me up. When I felt his tongue and fingers pull out of my holes, I knew he was about to take me over the edge!

He rubbed the tip of Mr. Big on my clit, dipped the head just inside the opening of my pussy, and pulled out. He then placed him at the entry to my asshole and my body twitched with anticipation of him entering my backdoor. He plunged inside my asshole and I squirted as I came from the feel of him.

"Yes!" I screamed in pleasure.

That match that was ignited was now a full fledge wildfire as Cooper fucked me fast and hard in my ass. I never knew getting fucked in the ass brought on so much pleasure. I felt like I was having an out of body experience, watching myself getting fucked by the love of my life. My orgasms kept coming one after another in a fit of rage, tearing through my body with no apologies. And when Cooper pulled my head up and back by my hair, I was done.

He was done. Cooper began calling my name over and over as he pumped in and out. I could feel him swell up as his nut came to a head. His balls slapped against my pussy as he fucked me senseless. Each slap of his balls, though, kept that spark shooting through me wanting more even when I knew I couldn't take anymore. But for this man, I was willing to be ridden until I passed the hell out and can longer remember my name.

Cooper called my name and professed his love for me as he shot his load up my ass. I could feel the warm liquid filling me up and sliding out of me as he stroked me until he had nothing left. He let my hair go and balanced himself on the wall with his hands to keep from falling over on me. I held onto the bench. We remained connected with his dick still in my ass while we caught our breath. Once we had our breathing back to normal, Cooper slowly pulled out of me and helped me up. I turned to face him and kissed him passionately.

"I love you," I said breaking our kiss.

"I love you too, ma. Now let's get the hell out of this cold ass water," Cooper replied.

I turned the shower off and we exited. We wrapped up in towels and made our way back to bed. Just as Cooper instructed, I called my assistant and told her to hold the fort down at the office because I would be working from home. Well, I will in a few more hours after this nap I'm about to take.

Chapter 6: Cozy Meal

Tonight, was supposed to be a lady's night out with my girls, Carla, and Shannon. We were going to attend this cooking class Shannon had been telling us about for the past couple of weeks. She raved on and on about the meal she prepared but more so the chef and how good looking he was. The way Shannon went on and on about the chef, I was sure she had more than a meal with him. I honestly thought she had an orgasm while she spoke to us about him.

That's why I was a bit agitated when she and Carla texted me at the last minute saying they wouldn't be able to make it to this cooking class. The Uber driver pulled up to what looked like an abandoned warehouse. The sign above the entrance read "Cozy Meal." Before getting out of the car I checked my surroundings making sure there wasn't anyone suspicious around. I did notice a couple of cars parked along the street. I assumed they were the other patrons attending the class.

Reluctantly, I got out the car and stood out front as I watched the Uber driver pull off and zoom down the dark road. I took a deep breath before entering the building. The hostess introduced herself as Lady and led me into an area that was arranged with eight cooking areas. I was astounded to find I was the only one there, seeing all the cars outside.

"Am I in the right place?" I turned to ask Lady, but she was no longer around. I went back into the receptionist area and it was empty. "What the hell is going on?" I plopped my hands on my hips.

I was beginning to believe this was some kind of set up. I pulled my phone out of my coat pocket and dialed Shannon's number. "Wassup, Maci! How's the class going?" she asked a little too chipper for me.

"What the hell is going on, Shannon? I'm the only one here at this place."

"Calm down, sis. This is for your own good." Shannon laughed and another female voice joined in. I knew it was Carla.

"What are you talking about and what's so damn funny?" I was pissed now, and these two tramps were getting a laugh on my expense.

"Maci just go with the flow. You will thank us later," Carla said, and the call ended.

"Ain't this a bitch!" I said aloud to no one in particular. I wasn't for the theatrics anymore. I pulled my phone back out and was strolling to the Uber app when my phone was snatched out of my hands.

"That won't be necessary," a deep, baritone voice said from behind me.

I jumped and took off running towards the door only to find it locked. I turned and shook the handle but to no avail; the door did not open. When I felt a hand on my shoulder, I screamed and blindly began swinging my fisted hands, only hitting air.

"Miss Wilson, please calm down!" the man called out.

After tiring myself out from swinging and not connecting to anyone nor anything, I gave up and put my hands down to my side and slowly opened my eyes. They landed on the most gorgeous man ever to walk earth. I don't remember ever being attracted to a man outside of my race, but this man standing before me had me feeling things I hadn't felt in long time.

To start, he was surprisingly tall for an Asian man. Typically, the ones I've encountered were all on the short side or at least shorter than what I'm attracted to. He looked to be right at six feet tall. His round face was gorgeous with dark, yet bright eyes, dimples that winked at me from the more gorgeous smile that had me on edge. My eyes continued to roam over his body and the muscles that bulged out from all the right places had me on the verge of climaxing. The way the white t-shirt fit across his chest told how fit he was.

"I didn't mean to scare you. I am Chef Darren Wong and your friends Shannon Pierce and Carla Mansoon told me you knew this would be a private session," he stood in place with hands up in surrender.

"Well, uh, no I didn't know! Those two heifers didn't tell me anything. And when I see them, I'm gonna kill 'em!" I said. Of course, I wasn't going to really kill them, but you bet your ass I was going to go in on them. They could have just told me it was a private session instead of being dramatic and I wouldn't be standing her looking like a crazed woman!

"My apologies to you. Well, you have me for the next couple of hours. What you say? Can we go cook something? I see no need to waste the time," Chef Wong said with sincerity.

I felt bad for how I was taking my anger out on him and decided to let the night continue. I waved my hand out for him to lead the way. I followed him back into the cooking area. We went over to the teaching area where he had salmon, yellow fin tuna, cooked shrimp, cucumber, avocado, rice, rice vinegar, seaweed salad, ginger, wasabi, eel sauce, and Japanese mayo; all things to make sushi. Somehow this didn't surprise me since my sneaky friends know how much I love sushi even though I've never actually made it.

"You can place your things over on that hook over there," Chef Wong pointed to a wall where several hooks were.

I did as instructed, then went back over to the set up. I washed my hands and grabbed the apron he held out for me. I pulled it over my head then to my surprise, Chef Wong was standing behind me, very close I might add, and tied the strings. "You're all set now," he said. I could feel his lips on my ear as he spoke.

"Oh, okay," was all I could muster up. All of a sudden, I felt heat rising from somewhere and I began fanning myself.

"First we have to cook the rice. While the rice is cooking, we'll cut up and mix the other ingredients," Chef Wong said running water into the rice cooker.

I stood by waiting for further instructions as he poured the rice into the rice cooker, then set it up on the countertop. He turned to me and we were face to face, so close I could feel his breath on my nose as he breathed in and out. My heart skipped a beat when he smiled, and those damn dimples popped out. My clit throbbed when the tip of his tongue swiped across his lips. Lawd, forgive me for I know I'm about to sin!

"So, your friends tell me sushi is your favorite dish," Chef Wong said.

"Huh?" I asked shaking my head. "What'd you say?" I had no idea I had zoned out.

"I said your friends tell me sushi is your favorite side dish."

"Oh, yeah. Yes, it is," I said breathlessly.

"Good! Let's get started preparing the ingredients." Chef Wong turned his attention to the items on the island and picked up the cucumber. My panties instantly became moist looking at the size of the cucumber in his hand and imagined it was his dick. I pictured him standing there naked stroking himself to full attention.

"We'll start off cutting up this cucumber. Why don't you step up and give me a hand," Chef Wong motioned with his head for me to come closer.

I slowly moved over to the island and took up the space next to him. I grabbed a cucumber in one hand and a knife in the other. I felt the heat rising again so I took a step to my right hoping to get some air flowing between us. I took in a deep breath to calm my nerves. "Okay, so tell me what to do."

"First, we cut the cucumber in half. Then cut them in half the long way. Once we cut them that way, we will then cut them into smaller pieces until we have a few strips," Chef Wong explained moving over so that he was standing right back next to me.

I followed his instructions as we prepared the sushi. Along the way we struck up a get-to-know-you conversation. I learned he was half Japanese and half Dutch American. His parents met at an art museum and some years later they were married. All throughout the class, Chef Wong would find some way to touch me, brush up against my ass or breast. The little actions had my pussy drooling at the lips and my clit throbbing. I honestly didn't know how much longer I'd be able to take being so up close and personal with this man.

We had finally finished rolling the sushi and placing it onto plates. I must say it looked delicious. As if on cue, my belly growled, ready to be filled with the appetizers I'd just help create. "Now that we've finished prepping, it's now time to enjoy," Chef Wong said.

"Good! My belly has no objections to that," I half-joked.

"Here, you take these to the table, and I'll grab some wine. Do you have a preference?" Chef Wong asked.

"Anything that's not red or bitter," I took the plates over to the table we set earlier. I took my apron off and hung it on one of the hooks.

"Did I tell you how sexy you look in this dress?" Chef Wong whispered in my ear. He was standing behind me with all of his business on my ass. His tongue flicked my earlobe causing me to gasp. He grabbed a hold of my left titty and gave it a squeeze.

"No, no you didn't," I managed to say. Shannon was very adamant I wore a dress and had even picked out the one I am wearing. It was a knee-length, quarter sleeve, burgundy dress with a plunging neckline. It fit my body like a glove. I was what society considered a full-figured woman. I had DDD breast, a small pudge, and an ass that was just as big, if not bigger, than my breasts. Standing at 5'8", I had thick long legs that made me look like an amazon. Who knew this Asian persuasion was into BBWs?

"Well, you are," Chef Wong said in between the kisses he was placing on my neck. He placed his hand inside my dress and pulled my titty out of my bra, playing with my large nipple. I moaned as it hardened to his touch. He pulled my dress up with his other hand and placed it between my thighs, rubbing on my wet pussy through the fabric of my panties. "You're so wet for me," Chef Wong crooned.

I backed my big ass into his hard dick that was poking on me through his pants. I moaned a little louder when he eased two fingers inside my pussy as his thumb rubbed my clit. My hips gyrated on his fingers thrusting inside my soaking pussy. I obliged him and pulled my dress up over my ass. I pulled my thong down and let it fall freely to the floor then stepped out of them.

Chef Wong pulled his fingers out of me and placed them in my mouth. I sucked my juices off his fingers enjoying my taste. He turned me to face him then planted a rough kiss on my lips, sucking ferociously on my bottom then top lips before plunging his tongue inside my mouth. I unbuttoned his pants and slid them along with his boxers down his legs. The head of his thick dick popped out and right at my pussy.

He stepped out of his pants then picked me up and carried me to the nearest island. He gently laid me down and spread my legs wide. He bent down and devoured my pussy into his mouth. I arched my back and pushed his face deeper into my pussy with a hand. "Ooh, umm," I moaned. I fucked his face as I played with my breast. I plopped one of my titties in my mouth and sucked on my nipple. This always turned the men on more when they saw me sucking my own titty. Chef Wong was no different.

He moaned in my pussy as he sucked on my clit while watching me intently. Watching him watching me is what turned me on, and I began to come all over his tongue. My juices spilled out down his chin and onto the island and the floor. My thick legs shook as my orgasmic waves ran through my body. Chef Wong stood and opened one of the drawers coming out with a condom. He tore the foil and wrapped the magnum on his large dick. He had a decent length, but it was the girth that called for a condom that came in the gold foil.

Once he had the condom down his shaft, he plunged in my pussy with no mercy. He placed my legs on his shoulders and went to work. He stretched my pussy so wide with his dick, I'm not sure my pussy will jump back to its normal size once he's done fucking me. But I be damn if the dick isn't good. I held onto the edge of the island and arched my back. I threw the pussy back on him with each stroke. "Ahh, yes, just like that," Chef Wong moaned.

Out of nowhere Lady appeared and was standing at my head. Her soft hands came to my breast and she pulled them both out of my bra and dress. She leaned over me and began sucking on them. So now, here I was in a threesome with two strangers and one of them being a woman. This was never something I would do but I can't say I'm not enjoying being the center of pleasure at this very moment. The mixture of her soft lips on my breast and his hard dick thrusting inside my pussy brought me to my second orgasm, and a very hard one at that.

"Aaaah shit, I'm coming!" My body jerked and twitched as Chef Wong continuously to stroke my g-spot. The sensation from Lady sucking my breast made my orgasm more intense. But when she moved from my breast and made her way to my pussy and sucked on my clit while Chef Wong fucked me, I was done. I gushed what felt like a rainfall as I came! I shouted out so loud, I swear the whole damn neighborhood heard me. This orgasm caused me to black out from the intensity.

When I gained consciousness, I realized I was in my bed at home. How the hell did I get back home? I tried to get up, but I was just too weak to move, and my head began to spin. Then my stomach growled letting me know I hadn't eaten since lunch yesterday. I laid my head back on the pillow. I heard voices outside of my bedroom door. It sounded as if they were arguing. I was just about to call out to them when the door opened. In walked Shannon and Chef Wong. They both looked as if they'd just been told some horrific news.

"Cami, are you all right? I'm so sorry this happened," Shannon said taking a seat on the bed.

I looked over at Chef Wong who looked genuinely concerned. Then I looked back at Shannon who looked like she was about to shit her pants. "I'm all right. But the next time you think it would be a good idea to spring a surprise on me, please don't."

Part 2: Blazing

Chapter 7: Broke Down

It's our anniversary. We decided at the beginning of the week we are going to drive down to the coast to celebrate. We were supposed to leave early this morning, but Johnathan was called in for an impromptu meeting. He assured me we'd be on the road by noon. However, it's now 7:30p.m. and we are just now leaving.

Johnathan insists on driving his old school Chevy Impala. I don't want to ride in that damn car because it's bound to break down and have us stranded on the side of the road in the middle of nowhere. But my man is adamant we were good to go since he had it serviced yesterday.

We are just crossing state lines when we hear a pop then fluid gushing out onto the windshield followed by smoke. The car sputters and clumps out as soon as Johnathan pulls over onto the shoulder of the road.

"Don't say anything, Erin," Johnathan says.

I don't even bother responding. I roll my eyes and cross my arms over my ample breasts. I look straight ahead with my lips poked out. Johnathan pops the hood and gets out of the car to take a look. I look around at my surroundings and there is not a car in sight. This road is pitch black and we are next to some woods. It looks like a scene from that movie "Wrong Turn," and it gives me the creeps.

I turn to face Johnathan when he gets back in the car. He looks over at me as if he didn't want to break the bad news to me or more so to tell me I'm right. "It's the radiator. I'm about to call a tow truck to get us to the nearest shop. I'm sorry, baby."

As much as I want to revel in the 'I told you so,' I don't want to add to the already fucked up situation. I know he just wants to be spontaneous in the moment and make this an unforgettable weekend. So instead I lean over and give him a long passionate kiss. "No worries my love. We just have to make the best of the situation at hand."

"See, that's why I married you," Johnathan pecks me on the lips once more before pulling up the AAA app and requesting roadside assistance.

After Johnathan requests AAA, we are just sitting quietly in our own thoughts when I decide to make the best of our situation. I lift up out of my seat just enough to pull my dress up and then over my head taking it off. Because it's a halter and I have perky breast I'm not wearing a bra. I pull my thong panties off and toss them over to Johnathan who's eyeing me the entire time I undress. I lean my back against the door and place my left leg between the console and seats giving him a full view of my clean-shaven pussy. I grab a breast with one hand and begin masturbating with the other.

Johnathan licks his lips then places his face between my thighs nudging my hand out of the way. He replaces my hand with his tongue twirling it around my now erect clit. He sucks my clit into his mouth, and I moan at the sensation. I arch my back and spread my legs further apart when he slides three fingers inside my hot box. "Mmm, that feels so good," I croon.

Johnathan licks up and down my pussy making a trail to my asshole. He circles his tongue around the outside of my asshole before slithering his tongue inside. He continues to thrust his fingers in and out of my pussy. I can feel my orgasm coming and I arch my back more. I place my hand on Johnathan's bald head and gyrate my ass and pussy brining myself to an explosive orgasm.

"Aah! Aah! Oh shit, baby!" I scream as I explode on his fingers. My asshole tightens around his tongue and I come again.

Johnathan licks my ass and pussy a few more minutes before he comes up for air. "I swear you taste sweeter every damn time," Johnathan says in between licking my juices off his fingers.

I sit up and suck his tongue into my mouth tasting my juices. I break away from the kiss and pull my leg back over so I'm sitting back straight. "Take your clothes off then meet me at the trunk of the car," I instruct Johnathan.

He scrunches up his face trying to see if I'm serious. I open the door and get out of the car to show him rather than tell him how serious I am. I don't wait to see if he will do as I instruct since I already know he will. A couple of minutes later and he climbs out of the car. He makes his way to the trunk. "Are you sure about this, babe?" Johnathan asks, looking around. He positions himself between my legs.

I lay back onto the windshield and spread my legs open into a split. Johnathan doesn't hesitate to pull me to the edge of the trunk and ease into my waiting, wet pussy. Just as he begins to stroke in and out of me it starts to pour down raining. "Oh shit, Erin. Fuck!" Johnathan lets out.

I meet him stroke for stroke throwing my pussy on his thick dick. Thunderclaps and lightning strikes through the sky as he strikes my g-spot effortlessly. "Oh baby, just like that!" I shout. My legs begin to shake as I begin to cream all over Johnathan's dick. The raindrops pounding down on my naked body along with him hitting my spot with every stroke has me coming back to back nonstop.

"I need to hit this from the back," Johnathan says pulling out of me.

He helps me down off the trunk and I turn my back to him. I place a leg on top of the hood and bend over anxiously waiting to be filled by him. Instead of entering my pussy, Johnathan enters my ass and I gasp aloud. The pleasurable pain I'm feeling is pure ecstasy. He grabs a hand full of my hair as he thrust in my ass. I reach between my legs and begin playing with my clit.

Car lights a distance out catches my attention. I begin popping my ass on Johnathan's dick, squeezing my anal muscles around his dick. I flick my finger faster on my clit bringing myself to yet another massive orgasm at the same time Johnathan begins to come in my ass. "Ooh shit, John. Na. Than!"

"Shit, Erin! Oh baby! Sss," Johnathan replies with grunts of pleasure.

He slaps my ass cheek as he pulls out of me. I take my leg down and we hurry back into the car before the car I'd seen earlier passes by us. We laugh at our spontaneous sexcapades as we dry ourselves off with the towels in one of the bags I'm thankful I placed in the back seat. It doesn't take me long until I'm fully dressed. Johnathan pulls his shirt over his head just as blue lights flash from the rear and a squad car pulls up behind us. We give each other a look that says, 'that was a close call' and laugh as the officer climbs out of his squad car. The officer approaches us on Johnathan's side of the car. He flashes his flashlight in both of our faces and in the back seat. "How you folks doing this evening?"

"We're fine, Officer. Our car broke down and we're just waiting for Triple A to arrive," Johnathan explains.

As on cue, a tow truck's yellow flashing lights can be seen in the rearview mirror. The driver pulls up in front of us and gets out. "Hey, Jimmy, you the Triple A for these folks here?' the officer asks the driver who looks like a younger version of him. I assume Jimmie is the officer's son.

"Yeah, Paw. I was out at the Kaminski's when I got dispatched," Jimmie replied.

"Well, let's get them hooked up and to the shop so they can be on their way." Jimmie nods his head at his father and gets to work hooking our car up to the trailer.

"I'll take y'all over to the Inn so you can get checked into a room for the night since your car won't be looked at until the morning," the officer tells us.

We grab our belongings and follow the officer to his squad car. So much for a relaxing, fun filled weekend on the coast. But we will always remember the night or car broke down.

Chapter 8: Thief in the Night

The night was coming to a close, and I am feeling the five glasses of vodka and cranberry drinks I had throughout the night. I am feeling bittersweet at the moment. Why you ask? Well I'll tell you. First, it's my thirtieth birthday, hence why it's a sweet moment. Second, my date is MIA, the reason for the bitter. I was supposed to be escorted by this tall glass of fine, brother who assured me I'd have the best birthday ever, but he had to cancel at the last minute. For the most part, my day has been great. It started off with a knock on my door from a courier delivering a huge bouquet of roses with a card attached. In it was surprise a full spa service that I later learned included a happy ending!

I quickly dressed and ran out of the house to get my spa services underway. I received a full body massage from this sexy ass masseuse who gave me the best tongue lashing I'd ever experienced at the same time this cute red head with green eyes gave me a facial. Mr. Masseuse also broke me off with some bomb ass dick. It felt amazing getting fucked and getting a facial done at the same time. It was something amazing not knowing what would happen next since my eyes were closed the entire time at one point,

Red halted the facial and gave my tits, twin peaks as I call them, some attention sucking on my nipples. I've never been into girl-on-girl action, but the feel of her soft lips latched onto my nipples as I got fucked had my orgasm more intense than usual.

After my spa services, I went to my favorite nail salon and got hooked up by my girl Bon. After being pampered all day, I arrived home and relaxed in a hot bath before it was time to get ready for my night. I had planned my thirtieth birthday bash a year ahead to make sure everything was in place. I reserved my favorite bistro and deejay. I had my outfit custom made by an up and coming designer. I even had my shoes custom made. My hair and makeup were done to perfection. To say I was feeling myself is an understatement. I was looking like and feeling like a superstar!

My five foot five, two hundred-pound, size fourteen bootylicious body turned heads as I stepped out of the limo and made my way up the purple carpet wearing a form-fitted, floor-length strapless purple dress. It shimmers with every step I take. I chose a purple instead of red since purple is my favorite color. At the entrance of the bistro was a backdrop for photos that held my custom-made logo that was a silhouette of my body in a seductive pose with my hair flowing in the wind. Along with my custom-made logo were the sponsors I negotiated deals within agreement that they would foot the bill for my extravagant party, and I would give them cameos in my next four book releases. It's always a win-win when you can make money while having a good time with your loved ones.

The party was lit, and I was feeling myself even more as the night went on. Family and even some friends came in from out of town to help me celebrate. As I was talking to my cousin, Tasha, about our next vacation, a fine, tall brotha with a mocha complexion caught my eye as he sauntered in looking like he'd just stepped off the pages of GQ Magazine. My kitty instantly began purring with want. My nipples hardened when he flashed a smile and winked at me.

"Damn, he is foine!" Tasha exclaimed.

"Yes, Lawd and he's going to be my ultimate birthday gift," I declared.

"If I wasn't a happily married woman, I'd be all over that! Umm!" We both laughed and high-fived each other.

For the remainder of the night, I am only able to toss flirtatious glances at Mr. GQ. It seems as if everyone could sense our sexual attraction towards each other. Every time either one of us tries to make our way over to the other, someone steps in our path and directs us away from each other for some odd reason. Now I'm becoming agitated by this shit but doing my best to keep my cool. It's a hard task especially being solo to my own dam party. But I don't want to cause a scene, most importantly when I have business associates present.

I finally say my goodbyes to all my guests, except Mr. GQ. It's now I realize he must have left some time ago while I was on the dancefloor doing the wobble since that is the last time, I remember seeing him. "Oh well," I say aloud as I slide into the back seat of my waiting limo.

Thirty minutes later, my driver pulls up alongside the curb in front of my house. I sigh as I look out the window at my gorgeous two-story brick home. Besides the porch light, there was no other light on in the house. I thank my driver and give him a hefty tip for his services before I make my way up the steps leading to the front door. I unlock the door and step inside. Just as I close the door and turn the lock, the front of my body is pressed against the door and a set of hands are all over my bodacious ass, griping, squeezing my plumpness.

A male voice groans in my ear and he press his hard penis into my backside. His warm breath smells of mint as his lips brush lightly against my ear. "I—" I only get out, but he shushes me. "Mmm," I moan when he bites down in the crook of my neck, sucking my skin into his mouth. He pulls the split of my dress open and easily finds my hot box since I'm not wearing any panties. His fingers lightly brush against my no throbbing pearl in a teasing manner. My pussy pulsates with excitement.

When he slides his fingers inside me, I immediately cream on them. Instinctively, I arch my back pushing my ass more into his erection. He obliges me and push his hard dick more into my ass as he finger fucks me to an orgasm. I cry out in pleasure of him massaging one of my titties and my pussy at the same damn time. I know I should be frightened right now but how can I when everything he is doing to me feels oh so good?

"Take me to your bedroom now," he says with authority. He pulls my head back with a hand full of my hair. He pulls his fingers out of me and puts them to my lips. I open my mouth and suck my juices off his fingers. I release his fingers from my mouth, and he steps back just enough for me to turn around.

When we are face to face, he slams his lips into mine before I can get a good look of his face. His tongue snakes inside my mouth when I gasp. He kisses me with so much passion and want. I feel like putty in his hands as I have a mini orgasm from his kiss. He has to tighten his embrace to hold me up. He finally pulls away from our kiss and I'm now able to get as good of a look as I can in the darkness. His big eyes brightly bare into mine. I still at them as if he just hypnotized me with his stare.

There's no light in my living room where we currently stand, but I am able to see the defined jawline of his facial feature. I can also tell that this man is handsome, one that always has the ladies' panties moist just off his looks alone. My mind is telling me I should be scared of this man, but I'm not. What I am is horny and ready to be taken by him like a thief in the night.

As if he senses what my mind is saying, he grabs me by an arm and shove me towards the staircase. I obey his nonverbal command and lead him upstairs to my bedroom. He pushes me onto the bed, and I fall face first onto my plush down comforter. I feel his hands on my back then my dress loosening as he pulls the zipper down. "Lift up," he commands.

I do as I am told, and he shimmies the dress from under me and tosses it onto the floor. He pulls my shoes off one by one, tossing them to the floor as well. Now I'm lying on my stomach butt ass naked, waiting, anticipating his next move. I can hear him removing his clothing and shoes. I want to turn around and get a good look at him and his dick but before I finally found the nerves to do so, his hands were on my ass, squeezing my cheeks and spreading them apart. "Get on all fours," he says.

I quickly get into his desired position and toot my ass to the ceiling. I feel his tongue run down my pussy lips and back up continuing to my asshole. I swirl my hips in pleasure as he eats my pussy and asshole, not knowing which way his tongue and mouth will go. I bury my face in the comforter making my moans muffle as they grew an octave. My legs begin to quake as my orgasm took over my body.

The more he licks and sucks my clit, the stronger my orgasmic wave slams through my body. I can feel my nectar running down the insides of my thighs from me raining down on his tongue. My knees buckle under me and I fall forward, but strong arm catches me and holds me in place. He sucks on my clit for several more minutes causing my body to twitch until he finally releases my clit from his mouth.

I don't have a chance to catch a breath before he fills me with his dick as he thrusts inside me. "Oh god!" I cry out from both pleasure and pain. I fist the comforter as he begins long but steady strokes, hitting my g-spot as he thrusts deeper until it feels like he is at my bottom.

"Mmm, baby. Just like that. Yeah, throw this pussy on my dick. Just. Like. That," he grunts out in between strokes. I toss my cookies back on him, throwing him a curve when I begin a counterclockwise twerk while tightening my pussy muscles around his massive dick. "Shit! Oh fuck!" he calls out.

His grip tightens on my waist as he picks up the pace, now trying to keep up with me. I can tell he is on the verge of coming from how loud his grunts are getting with every stroke. I, however, am not quite ready to end this fuck session so I pull away from him so that he slips out of me. "What are you doing?" he asks confused by my actions.

"It's my turn," I ooze with seduction. I shove him down onto the bed and straddle him. I grab ahold of his dick and position him at my opening. I slide down on him with ease since I was already dripping from my previous orgasms. I lean forward so that we are chest to chest, and I begin bouncing on his dick, tightening around him as I come up and releasing as I come down.

He grabs my hips trying to control the pace as he fucks me back but I ain't having that. Yeah, he originally came in taking my goodies, but now he's getting fed them by me. Throwing my juicy pussy on him, I position myself just so the right amount of friction hits my clit. I can feel us both at our peaks and we climax simultaneously. "Oh shit!" we both yell in unison. I continue to ride him until he is flaccid.

I roll over onto the bed, but he pulls me right back on top of him. "Damn, baby! This was the best sex we've had in quite some time!" Tyrone exclaims. "I didn't think I'd be into it, but this role-playing shit is the bomb!"

"Yeah, bae. It sure is," I agree. "Tasha said role playing would take our love making to a whole other level and she was definitely right. From the spa earlier to the build up to now, I had to hold back from getting ghost to get myself off before I could get home to you. And it didn't help how sexy you were looking tonight."

Tash and her husband, Rick, had been telling us for quite some time that Tyrone and I should try role playing here and there. They both swore by it, but we were apprehensive. We finally decided to give this thing a try since our businesses had been taking away a lot of our attention from each other. Realizing that, all week we kept our distances from each other acting as if we were strangers, wanting to make tonight more intriguing. Tyrone paid my favorite spa to rent the place out today so that while he was giving me my "massage," other patrons wouldn't here our moans ricocheting off the walls. We also decided on the stranger in my house role play because Tyrone and I like it rough every now and then. I'm so glad we took my cousin and her husband's advice.

Feeling my man's dick growing hard underneath me, I slide down between his legs and take him in my mouth, tasting the mixture of our fluids. From then on, my husband and I made love and fucked each other until we saw daylight.

Chapter 9: Justified

I sat across the courtroom from my soon to be ex-husband, Mario, waiting for the judge to enter. Even now as we sit here, I can't believe we're getting a divorce. I never in a million years thought we'd end up here, here in a courtroom, here at divorce court! This is insane.

Why are we here is the real question though. We actually had just made love before we even stepped foot onto this property this morning. Both Mario and I professed our love to each other a mere two and a half hours ago! So, I'm at a total loss right now.

The double doors behind us opening bring me back into the moment. Then the answer to my question walks in wearing a black pencil skirt, a black sheer button-down shirt, black stilettos, and a face that is a replica of mine. My half-sister Amena saunters in as if she owns the place and takes up one of the empty seats behind Mario. Not once does she look my way.

It saddens me that she is this way with me. We literally can pass for twins. If you think about it, in some ways we actually are. We are born on the same day exactly one minute a part, me being the oldest. We have the exact same face, down to the small mole that sits just above our lip on the right side. We have the same green-gray eyes and naturally long curly hair. We both took our looks after our father. The two differences between Amena and I are that we have different mothers. My mom is married to our dad, while her mom was his side piece at the time.

Our dad didn't give a shit about that though. He made it clear to both our mothers that he wanted us to grow up and be close. He never allowed us to say we were half-sisters. If he heard us speak any differently about each other, he would go into a tirade. So, for his sake, and until I caught her in bed with my husband, we put on the false pretenses.

The day I caught my husband in bed with my sister, I let all the build up from over the years of dealing with that conniving bitch unleash and I beat her ass into a coma. Hell, I damn near set his ass on fire and would have had he not been able to make it inside the bathroom and turn the shower on. What kept me from being locked up in jail was Mario. He refused to press charges and he somehow convinced Amena not to do the same. At the time I didn't care what would happen to me because my life as I knew it was over anyway.

So now here we are, waiting for the judge to come and give us his verdict on the terms of the prenup we'd signed before saying I do. Being that we both had our own businesses and assets before getting together, we wanted to make sure we had provisions in place to protect them if we were to ever find ourselves in the predicament we're currently in now. Another part of the prenup states that if there was infidelity by either party, that person would have to pay alimony, cover court fees, and give up the house we'd purchase together. Since Mario was the one to cheat and is still fucking Amena, she wants him to contest the prenup and go after me. She claims she has proof that I cheated. But what she did was pretend to be me and record herself fucking the guys in the videos.

"All rise. The honorable Judge Jason Miles is presiding," the bailiff calls out.

We all stand, and I'm taken aback at the judge. He is younger than most judges I've seen and extremely handsome. He isn't too tall, but I can tell he's still taller than me even if I were in my six-inch stilettos. Well, being that I'm exactly five feet tall, just about anyone would be taller than me anyway. Anyway, Judge Miles has a smooth milk chocolate complexion and I wonder if his magic stick is the same color. My mouth waters and my kitty pulsates at the thought of how delicious he would taste. As I stand here watching him, I run my hand down the front of my white floral knee-length dress that doesn't need to be smoothed out since it fits my curvaceous body like a glove.

I am delighted when my movement caught his eye and he looked over at me. I can see the lust in his eyes before he looked over to Mario's side of the room. "Please be seated." My breath got caught in my throat at the sound of Judge Miles's soothing baritone voice and for a moment after everyone else was seated I remain standing.

"Ahem," my lawyer, Frederick, places a hand on my arm to get my attention.

"Oh, I-I'm sorry," I say looking embarrassed.

"No worries. So, we're here today to finalize the divorce settlement and to make a ruling on the prenuptial agreement between Mario Dante

115

Dawson and Alexandria Renee Dawson," Judge Miles says. "Before I make my ruling, though, I want to speak privately and separately with you Mr. Dawson and you Mrs. Dawson."

I look to Frederick to see if he would object and both he and Mario's attorney jump up at the same time and yell their objections, which Judge Miles over rules just as quick. Mario hesitantly stands up and makes his way to the judge's chambers. I keep my poker face on as I sit waiting for Mario to come out of the judge's chambers. The entire time Frederick is barking orders to his assistants to look up cases that he can throw at the judge if he comes with any shenanigans after my turn with him.

Twenty minutes later, Mario comes out and heads back to his seat. I can't tell either way if his talk with judge Miles was good or not. I stand and make my way to speak with Judge Miles when the bailiff calls my name. As soon as I am in his chambers and the door is closed, I turn around so Jason can unzip my dress. I am wearing this dress just for him since he purchased it for me a few weeks ago while we were out of town for a weekend getaway. He told me then that he was going to fuck me in his chamber just before he gave the ruling out in my favor.

He undid his robe to reveal he was already naked from the waist down and hard, ready for me. I drop down to my knees and took him into my mouth. Oh yes, his magic stick is that same mocha complexion as the rest of his body and if anyone was to say he didn't taste like chocolate, I'd slap the shit out of them for telling lies. I sucked and slurped his dick until he exploded in my mouth, which never takes long since my head game is sick. I also take no time sucking him back to a hard state.

I stand and go over to the leather sofa that sits along the long wall and lay on it. I placed my right leg over the top and beckon Jason with a finger. He hurries over to me and gets down on his knees and buries his face in my hot, wet pussy, lapping up my juices that trickle out of my canal and onto his tongue. He too has a mean head game, and within a couple of minutes, I am whimpering from my first orgasm.

Usually Jason would eat my pussy and suck my clit until I had at least three orgasms before he enters me, but today, right now, we don't have that kind of time. But later tonight, oh how we will get down! Jason climbs on top of me and thrusts deep inside me. To masks our moans, he plants his lips on mine and we kiss as he quickly pumps in and out of me. I meet him thrust for thrust and within in ten minutes we both have our second orgasms. This is the first time since we began this love affair three years ago that we actually had a quickie.

Yes, you are reading this right! Three damn years! You see, Mario and Amena have been fucking around on me since before we got married. I had been knowing about those two all along. The reason I stayed in this shitty ass relationship was to make sure I was able to get everything from him when I was able to gain control of his company, Dawson Solutions. Another part of the prenup that was outlined was that if we remained married for at least five years and I had a baby, I would get full control of his company if he was to cheat.

This is why Amena had him contesting the prenup. His dumbass nor his attorney caught that clause I had put in at the very last minute. Mario was just too eager to sign thinking he had a one up on me by adding that I had to give him a baby within the first two years or he could get everything. He tried his best to avoid having sex with me, but I pulled an Amena on him and pretended to be her. That night I got pregnant and the day I delivered our son Marcus James, I made sure to have a paternity test done.

After Jason and I are back in our clothes, I did a once over to make sure neither he nor I look disheveled before we go back into the courtroom. I'm so glad I wore clear lip gloss and not the pink shimmer one I started to. I made sure my hair was in it natural curly state so no one could tell if my hair was out of place. Giving Jason a quick peck on the lips, I open the door and make my way back to my seat. I keep my head down and look as if I'm disturbed by what Jason and I talked about.

"What did he say?" Frederick asks. I shake my head and wave him off as if I'm upset.

Jason steps back into the courtroom a few minutes later and plop down at the podium. He slaps his folder on top then opens it. He reads over the contents before looking up. "The prenuptial agreement that both parties have is binding. Mr. Dawson, you committed adultery against your wife and per the prenuptial agreement that you signed, you are to give up the house that you both resided at during your marriage. You are to pay Mrs. Dawson the agreed amount of $1,500 a month in alimony for six months beginning the first of next month. You are to cover all court costs and attorney fees. You also give up full control of Dawson Solutions since Mrs. Dawson kept to the agreement of giving birth to your son Marcus James Dawson within the first two years of your marriage. This therefore grants you both your divorce."

"Your honor, may I say something?" I abruptly ask before he hit the gavel.

"Sure," Jason says.

"Well, it's more of a request," I correct myself.

"Okay, and what would that be?"

"To legally go back to using my maiden name, Alexandria Blackwell," I look over to Mario and Amena. He looks like he is about to end his life while Amena now looks uninterested in him. She looks more disgusted than anything.

"Very well. Let the record show that Alexandria Dawson is now back to Alexandria Blackwell. Court is now adjourned." Jason hit the gavel and we all stood as he called court over.

"Now what was said that he wanted to speak to you privately about?" Frederick asks being nosey as hell.

"Let's just say he was making sure everything I received was justified," I wink at him and we laugh as we make our way out of the courtroom and out of the building. I am on my way to starting my new life over. But first, I have an appointment to take some legal dick-tations.

Chapter 10: Doctor's Orders

It's Melanie Jackson's first day on the job as a registered nurse at Piedmont Medical Center in New York. She just moved from the dirty south up to the big apple after losing both her parents in a six months' time frame. Her father dying from a heart attack, then her mom from what Melanie calls a broken heart of not having the love of her life at her side anymore. Melanie couldn't stand to be in her small town of Columbus, MS anymore so she did what Eddie Murphy's character in the movie Coming to America did and that was flip a coin to see if she would be heading North or West. Besides with her parents no longer here, she no longer had any immediate family being that she was an only child and she didn't have a family of her own at the moment.

Well the coin toss landed on heads, so North it was. But then the question came to what state would she make her new start in? D.C., Maryland, Philly, or New York were her top choices. After thinking over her options for several days, she decided on New York, the city that never sleeps. She got online and began her job search. Being a Registered Nurse,

Melanie knew it wouldn't be hard for her to land a job. She just wanted to make sure she landed the right job at the right hospital.

She had been to New York a few times to visit her college roommate, Shante, who was also a Registered Nurse. Then it hit her. Why not reach out to Shante to see if there were any openings at the hospital she works at? At least she would actually know someone at work and someone she can hang out with on her days off. Melanie picked up the phone and called Shante. That phone call turned out to be the thing to make her finally smile in a long time. That one phone call landed Melanie a job right then and there. Shante had her fax her resume over to her while they were on the phone chatting. When the fax came through, Shante personally walked it over to her Nurse Supervisor and handed Melanie's resume along with her cellphone to her to do an interview over the phone.

After hanging up from that phone call, it was as if someone had pressed the fast forward button on the DVD player. She submitted her two-weeks resignation letter notice to her supervisor, got the information from Shante to the apartment building she lives in to get the hookup on her own apartment, and hired a moving service. Since she was living with her parents in the house they bought and paid off, Melanie put it up for sale and being in the great condition it was in, she had no problem getting an offer on the house.

Within one month, Melanie was now starting her life as a New Yorker and already humping it on the job with the traumas coming into the ER back to back. A stabbing victim, a gunshot victim, a young girl who suffered broken bones and bruised after being jumped on by several girls, and then a man who got a clit tickler stuck in his ass; yes, Melanie's first day on the job was a dozy. But with all that going on, it was the ER doctor she had been assigned to for the day that had her head spinning.

Doctor Randall Schaffer was the sexiest man to walk earth in Melanie's eyes. He was brown skinned with a low curly fade, clean shaven babyface, and stood at about six feet tall. From what she'd been told by Shante, he was thirty-two, divorced, and still single. Shante however couldn't stand him because he was always barking orders to her as if her job wasn't just as important as his. But the real truth was that Dr. Randall turned down her as well as all the other women staff and even some of the men's advances. Before it was known that some of the openly gay men made it known they tried to get with him, Shante had dubbed him to be gay since no man could resist her beauty. But once it was known he was turning the men down as well; they began to call him the Nazi because of his standoffish demeanor.

"Don't even waste your time on him. He'll turn you down just as well," Shante told her as they sat in the breakroom finally eating their lunch.

Melanie had been staring at Dr. Randall from the time he walked into the breakroom. She sat daydreaming about tearing off the scrubs and doctor's coat he wore and fucking him on the table she was sitting at eating her grilled chicken Caesar wrap. She was so into the daydream that she hadn't realized he was standing in front of her at that very moment.

"Melanie, is it?" Dr. Randall asked. Shante had to elbow her to bring her back into the moment.

"Huh?" Melanie looked bewildered. She blinked and looked over at Shante then up at the figure standing in front of her that she finally realized was him.

"Hi, Melanie. We haven't had a chance to really talk since it was in go mode as soon as we clocked in," Dr. Randall said.

"Oh, yeah. No, we haven't, but it's fine. It comes with the territory, you know," Melanie babbled on.

"True, but since we have some time, I'd like for us to chat and get to know each other since we will be working closely. Do you mind if we go to my office?"

Shante's mouth fell open. Since when did Doctor Randall Schaffer hold a conference with a new employee? Never! Not once had he even approached another employee about anything unless it was to tell them how incompetent he or she was. All of a sudden Shante begin to feel a bit jealous of her friend, and that was never something she'd ever had a trait of.

Melanie looked to her friend for assistance, but when she saw the expression on Shante's face, she didn't bother. She shook her head and stood. "Sure. Lead the way." Melanie took the other half of her wrap and placed it back in her lunch bag before placing the bag back inside the refrigerator.

Melanie and Dr. Randall walked to his office gaining stares from the staff as they passed them. They were speculating Melanie was in some type of trouble because she didn't do something to his specifications and being, she was the new kid on the block he didn't want to chastise her in front of everyone on her first day. Little did they know, they were so far from the truth.

Dr. Randall had been having a hard time getting through the day working closely with Melanie. As soon as he laid eyes on her, he rocked up and had been hard all damn day. She was gorgeous to him. Her slim frame, chocolate skin, and big doe eyes had him at hello. No, she didn't have a big ass or even big breast, but it really wasn't that for him. It was her whole aura that tugged at his heart string in just the five hours of her being in his presence. And her scent was divine to his nostrils. She smelled of vanilla and lavender, a combination that had him wanting to lick her from head to toe and back up.

In his office, Dr. Randall sat behind his desk across from Melanie who sat in one of the leather chairs. For a while they sat gazing into each other's eyes. Melanie could feel her panties getting wet and her nipples hardening. She licked her lips that seemed to feel dry all of a sudden and Dr. Randall's eyes bucked at the sight. "I have to be honest with you. I'm direct and I hope what I'm about to say don't cause you to want to go to HR on me. But I want you, Melanie. I want to make love to you right here, right now and then again after shift."

"Wow," Melanie said. She didn't know what to say or how to feel. She had never had a man be so blunt with her. All she could do was just stare at him. For several minutes she let his words play over and over in her mind. Finally, she stood and walked over to the door and locked it. She turned back to face him, and a smile slowly crept upon her face. "Dr. Randall, I'd rather show you than tell you what I think about what you just told me."

Melanie began to undress, first footing her shoes off, then pulling her scrub top over her head and off. Dr. Randall stood and began to undress as well. They watched each other undress until they were both naked. Melanie gasped at the size of his dick. She wondered if he will fit inside her. She'd had only two other lovers in her thirty years, and they were nowhere near his size or length. However, she was willing to give it a shot and take whatever she could.

Dr. Randall admired her beauty. She was what they call slim-thick. He liked how her areolas looked like chocolate kisses that he couldn't wait to latch onto. Her B-cup breast were perky, and he could tell she had a small but plump ass he couldn't wait to smack. They slowly walked towards each other and began kissing. He picked her up and hoisted her on his desk, standing between her legs.

"We have to be as quiet as possible even though my office is on the end of the hall," he told her between sucking on her breast. Then he stopped and looked up at her. "Once we do this, there's no going back."

"I know so shut up and fuck me before we get called back to the ER," Melanie said. She reached between them and grabbed his dick. She rubbed the head up and down the folds of her pussy lips then smacked it against her erect clit. Her juices spilled on the tip as his precum dripped out.

Dr. Randall gently shoved her so that she was lying flat on the desk. He then placed her legs on his shoulders. "Put him in," he grunted. Melanie guided his dick inside her tunnel hissing as he entered her. She voluntarily spread her legs wider trying to accommodate and adjust to his size. Feeling how tight she was, Randall pulled out and eased back in several times until he was finally all in.

"Wait. Just wait a second," Melanie said. It felt as if he'd ripped her a new hole, he was just that damn big. After some of the pain subsided, she nodded for him to continue. He slowly began thrusting in and out. After a few strokes, the pain turned into pleasure and Melanie was meeting him with thrusts of her own.

Randall picked up the pace and they got into a sexual vibe of love making. Melanie pulled his face down to hers and kissed him, sucking on his tongue and lips. He picked her up off the desk and walked her over to the wall and pressed her back to it. She bounced up and down on his dick, riding to her first orgasm. Her legs went numb as she gushed on his dick. She bit down in his chest to suppress her screams of pleasure.

He grunted at how tight, wet, and hot her pussy felt around his dick. He pumped harder and faster, not knowing if he would be able to hold out too much longer. He wanted to smack her ass when he came inside of her, so he placed her on her feet and turned her around. Melanie bent over and grabbed her ankles. Randall plummeted inside her and she squeaked. "Shh, baby," he said and smacked her on the ass.

Melanie pushed back into him feeling him at the bottom of her pussy and deep in her soul as he fucked her from behind. As much as either of them tried to keep quiet, the task was becoming harder to do so with him hitting her spot with each stroke and her wetness coating his dick like a hurricane raining down on the coast of Florida. Their moans and groans smacked off the walls in between his balls smacking her clit.

Melanie placed her hands on the wall and bounced on his dick as another orgasm began to take over her body. "Oh shit! Doc-doctor! Oh shit! I'm coming!" she squealed as her orgasm shot through her in a rush.

It felt as if she was about to pee when she began coming. Her juices shot out around him and down their legs. She looked down at the huge puddle between them and couldn't believe it.

Randall was on cloud twenty at that and his nut shot out of him so hard and fast he had to place his hands on the wall above Melanie to keep from falling on her. "Shit, Melanie! Fuck girl!" he groaned out in pleasure. His nut kept going as if it would never end. It was spilling out of her along with her juices, hitting the floor making a splatter sound in the puddle.

"Melanie, damn, baby. Shit," Randall sputtered.

"Yep, same here," Melanie agreed knowing exactly what it was he was trying to say. That was some great sex they'd just experienced.

It had been three years for Melanie and a year and a half for Randall. It had been that long since they'd been in relationships. This was the first time either of them had felt anything for anyone since their previous relationships. They both knew they had found their one and at that very moment they didn't care who was to find out about them.

Randall pulled out and away from Melanie. He took a step back and stood there in amazement at the woman before him. She smiled at him then stepped around their love puddle and up to him. She got down on her knees and took him in her mouth. Even with him being flaccid, he was still on the large side. She didn't care though. All she knew was that she wanted some more of this big dick and would do what need to be done to get him back hard. She slurped and licked his shaft, taking as much of him as she could, gagging in the process. She pulled him out with a pop then latched onto his balls as she gave him a hand job. She sucked and slurped his balls, moaning on them. He squirmed from the vibration and hissed out.

Melanie moved passed his balls and licked his asshole. He jerked from her in surprise. He'd never had his asshole licked and didn't know if he was down with that. However, he did notice how hard his dick got from it. His veins looked 3D at how much they were bulging. "Sit down. I want to ride now," Melanie instructed.

Randall sat on the sofa. She was about to straddle him with her back to him, but he bent her over and ran his tongue along her pussy. He ate her out from the back and even licked her asshole, returning the favor. When she squirted on his tongue, he drank her juices then sat back on the sofa so she could do her thing. Melanie straddled him and eased down on him. She twerked her ass on his dick as if she was dancing to a Luke song. "Sss, mmm, Mel—" Randall let out.

"Aah, yes, yes," she replied. She bounced up and down, fast then slow, clockwise, and counterclockwise until they both exploded together.

They'd just finished cleaning themselves up with the wipes and towels he kept in his office for those nights he pulled an all nightery when a page came over the hospital intercom for him. "Dr. Schaffer to the ER. Dr. Schaffer to the ER."

"Your place or mine after work?" he asked.

"Yours."

"I'll text you my address."

"Cool. I'll need to go home anyway and grab some clothes."

"Don't make me wait too long for you to make it over."

"I won't since those are the doctor's orders."

They shared a short but passionate tongue kiss before they were back off to the hustle and bustle of the ER trauma until their shift ended for the day.

Chapter 11: Sexting

"Candy, who is this guy you've been chatting with? What's his name? What does he look like?" Shanell barked off question after question.

"Why you so damn nosey?" Candy laughed.

"I need to know because he got yo ass glowing these days. I haven't seen my friend like this in a long time. So, tell me, who is he?"

"Uggh, you make me sick some damn times. I swear! But his name is Verdell. He's an engineer and I-I don't exactly know what he looks like," Candy admitted.

"Huh? How the hell don't you know what he looks like? So, what y'all met online or something?" Shanell was confused as hell. As much as Candy had been going on about this new guy, she assumed the bitch at least knew what he looked like.

"One day I mistakenly sent a text message to his phone that was intended for Jevar. I was a digit off on the numbers. Verdell texted me back and it just started from there." Candy shrugged.

"So, you broke up with Jevar for a guy that you've only been texting with back and forth? That is the dumbest shit, Candy."

"Bitch, first of all I broke up with Jevar because I caught his ass in bed with Sharee's dirty pussy ass! Of all the bitches to fuck, that bastard fucked the town hoe! And you know I ran my ass to the clinic to make sure I hadn't caught anything behind that shit."

"Oh well, you got a point there. I would beat both their asses for that. Okay, so then why are you just texting this dude and not actually seeing him? Those must be damn good texts."

"He has asked us to meet up, but I'm scared to."

"Why?"

"I'd hate to meet him and then he turns out to look like a dog and alien mix or he catfish me. Besides, after this fiasco with Jevar I'm not quite ready to jump into anything with anyone."

"So, you just gonna live off sexting and a damn vibrator?" Shanell laughed and Candy joined in.

"Shit for now, yea."

.... later that evening

Verdell: Hey beautiful. Wyd

Candy: Hey u! Just stepped out the shower

Candy: wyd hwyd

Verdell: Thinking bout u...just got home

Verdell: wish u were here wit me

Candy: ikr u could help me dry off

Verdell: fr fr I wanna see u, touch u, kiss u, feel u

Candy: oh my word

Verdell: I mean er' word ma

Candy: how are u feeling

Verdell: tired...not getting a lot of sleep

Candy: If I were there, I'd rock u to sleep

Verdell: I don't need u to rock me to sleep

Verdell: I need u to keep this head hard

Candy: I can do both

Verdell: and squirt on it...can u do that

Verdell: I will help

Candy: hmm never been a squirter but a creamer

Candy: but I'm always up for a challenge

Verdell: yes yes yes ma

Candy: look don't be talking that shit to me and I can't come home to it after being at work all day

Verdell: lol

Candy: don't laugh I'm serious lol

Verdell: shit tonight may be the night u skeet like never b4

Candy: but u r not here to make that happen

Candy: see now I'm horny and u not here at attention waiting for me to come say hello

Candy: and I need that right now

Verdell: I need to see it too

Verdell: will u let me squeeze ur booty

Verdell: I'll let u touch me...

Verdell: wherever u want

Candy: is that right

Verdell: yes

Candy: so, squeezing my boot is all u want to do

Verdell: if I'm allowed any special privileges then

Verdell: I won't turn them down

Candy: I'm sure u won't

Verdell: oh, u sure?

Verdell: really

Candy: of course

Verdell: I see

Candy: I don't normally toot my own horn, but beep beep

Verdell: I hear your horn

Candy: you wanna honk it for me

Verdell: yes, if u let me

Candy: mmm

Verdell: I'll push the button with my tongue

Candy: tell me more

Verdell: I just want to take your legs and put them on my shoulders

Verdell: and dive in face first into ur sweet pussy.... lick and suck until u can't take no more

Candy: ooh I can feel ur tongue on my hot box

Verdell: shit Candy when u gonna meet up wit me so we can turn this n2 a reality

Candy: iono 2 b honest.... how will I know if it's really u

Verdell: come on ma.... if a nigga come up 2 u wit the texts, we been doin

Verdell: then that muthafuka tapped n2 my shit

Verdell: tell me the real reason u don't want to meet me

Candy: 4 all I know u could be a serial killer, or some kind of psycho

Verdell: lmao but u been sexting me all this time ma

Candy: I know that seems cray, but I enjoy our sexting

Verdell: I know u ain't a virgin based off the first text u sent me by mistake

Candy: no, I'm not but after my breakup I'm just in chill mode

Candy: this has been keeping me afloat is all

Verdell: trust me ma I'll have u afloat, on top, above, n da dam air if that's what u want

Candy: lol

Verdell: we both grown…. let's cut the bullshit and meet up…if u change ur mind after then cool

Candy: ok…I guess we can do this

Verdell: come to this address 2nite….777 Lexington Dr

Candy: r u serious? That's n Pioneer Ct…. that's where celebrities live

Verdell: ma I know where I live…. just come to that address at 8

Candy: ok but I'm not coming alone…. I'm bringing my homegirl just n case u on some cray cray

Verdell: rotflmao if that makes u feel better then cool…c u l8r

Candy clicked on recent and dialed up Shanell. She answered on the first ring. "Bitch get dressed and come go with me to meet Verdell," Candy ordered.

"Oh, so you finally agreed to meet him, huh?"

"Yes and check it. He lives in Pioneer Ct."

"Un un, you are lying," Shanell said sounding skeptical and a little jealous.

"Well it's the address he gave me. Put on some damn clothes. I'll be at your house in thirty," Candy said and hung up.

She was so glad she'd just showered so all she had to do was oil her body and toss her clothes on. She chose a blue tennis dress and a matching lace panty and bras set. She slid her feet into a pair of thong sandals, grabbed her purse, phone, and keys before heading out of the door. Since she had such a gorgeous face, she didn't wear makeup and she always let her natural long hair do its own thing. She felt no reason to do anything differently than her normal routine. Either Verdell will take her as she was or not at all.

She was nervous about finally meeting Verdell face to face. She really hoped he wasn't on some psychotic bullshit. All that shit he had been talking via sext messages the past four months had been leaving her sexually frustrated and her dildos just weren't doing it for her anymore. Candy was craving the touch of a man, the feel of a man's body on hers, a real dick inside of her.

Exactly thirty minutes later, Candy sat in front of Shanell's house honking the horn of her Audi. Shanell came out of the house looking as if she had just stepped of the runway, wearing a maxi dress that flowed with each step she took, a pair of wedges, and make up done to perfection. Like Candy, Shanell was gorgeous without makeup but that didn't stop her. She never left out of her house without a full face done. She didn't have natural long hair like Candy, but she kept her weaves done as if she was a celebrity herself.

"Let's go meet Mr. Verdell," Shanell said once she was seated next to Candy in the car.

Candy pulled off and drove to the address Verdell gave her following the directions of the GPS. Within forty-five minutes she was pulling up the gate of the address she was given. She pushed the call button and a deep voice answered. "Candy, I see you are Miss Johnny on the Spot," the man chuckled.

"You said eight, right?"

"I did. Come on in." The gate buzzed, then the swung open. Candy slowly pulled forward and followed the brick driveway around until they came up to this mini mansion set on acres upon acres of land.

"Damn, bitch! You done hit the fucking jackpot!" Shanell exclaimed. Both of their mouths were open, and their eyes were bucked at the site before them. This was old money, not that type of money where someone had just hit the mega millions type of money. Whoever this Verdell character is was from a bloodline of old school money. The house was brick with a large porch, beautiful manicured landscape around it. There were several cars that sat in the front that range from and old school Chevy, Mercedes Benz, Range Rover, Porsche, and a Lamborghini.

"Girl don't get your hopes up. Verdell could be the help," Candy said. She didn't want to get her expectations up. She pulled her Audi up behind the old school Chevy and shut the car off. All of a sudden, she had butterflies in her stomach. She questioned what she was wearing and worried that she probably should have put on makeup and really did something to her hair. She reached over in her glove box and pulled out her brush and began brushing her hair so that it looked more presentable.

"Candice don't worry. You look fine," Shanell assured her. "Trust me, he is going to love everything he sees," she patted Candy on her leg.

Candy returned the brush back inside the glove box just as the front door to the house opened up. A tall light-skinned man, who could pass for a white guy stepped out onto the porch. He was very tall with an athletic build. His broad shoulders and bulky muscles stretched the black t-shirt he wore. His baggy sweatpants left nothing to the imagination as both women zoomed in on the large bulge in the center of his crotch. "Damn," they both said in unison.

Candy shot Shanell a dirty look and Shanell looked sheepishly. "Hey, I'm sorry, sis, but he got his shit out for a bitch to see and dammit I'm gonna look," Shanell told the truth. Candy couldn't be mad at that since she would have been doing the same thing had the roles been reversed. "But he looks familiar to me."

"Yeah, he does to me, too. I just can't place from where, though," Candy agreed.

The man stepped off the porch and walked to the car. He opened the door for Shanell first. "Good evening, ma'am," he greeted Shanell then hurried over to Candy's side and caught the door she'd just opened for herself. He stuck his hand out for her to grab as she climbed out of the car.

"Good evening to you, Miss Candice. Mr. Verdell is expecting you. Please follow me."

Candy was rather disappointed that he wasn't Verdell. But Shanell was smiling ear to ear at the revelation. Shit she could care less that he wasn't Verdell. As fine as this guy was, she was very much down to give him a ride. The ladies followed the man inside of the house into a foyer. The house was just as immaculate inside as it was outside with a huge crystal chandelier hanging from a tall ceiling, perfectly shined marble floors, grand staircase, and expensive vases filled with exotic floral arrangements that let off a sweet scent throughout.

"Mr. Verdell is waiting for you in the dining room," the man said.

He escorted the ladies to the dining room. As soon as they entered, both ladies gasped. Verdell was the Bryant Verdell Mcintosh of Mcintosh Conglomerated. He was just named Forbes' Richest Bachelor. Yes indeed, Candy had hit the jackpot because Verdell was indeed fine and rich! He actually resembled the man who'd escorted them in, looks and build.

Verdell stood and came over to the ladies. He walked right up to Candy and gave her a hug. He kissed her cheek before letting her go. "Hey, Candy. You look gorgeous. And you must be Shanell," Verdell said holding his hand out to Shanell. She took it and they shook hands.

"I am."

"Welcome to my home, ladies. This is my younger brother, Bradford."

"Hi," they ladies sang in unison.

"Since you told me you would be bringing Shanell I asked Brad to come over and keep her company. I hope you don't mind," Verdell said to them.

"Oh, no, it's not a problem at all," Shanell quickly stated. "Come on, Brad and give me a tour while these two lovebirds get acquainted."

Candy rolled her eyes. Shanell could be embarrassing sometimes and right now Candy was feeling just like that. Candy and Verdell watched as Shanell walked over to Brad and placed her arm around his. He smiled down on her and saluted the two as he escorted her out of the dining room. The entire time though, Verdell kept his eyes planted on Candy. She was more beautiful than her pics on her Facebook page.

After that first text message she sent him by mistake, he had her number looked up to see who it came from. Once he had a name, he did a search on her. He was happy to know she didn't have a criminal record and that she was beautiful. After getting a full background check on her, he finally responded to her text, well, sext message and things led them to the here and now.

Candy fidgeted with her purse strap. She was very nervous to be in his presence. Who thought the wrong number would lead her into a billionaire's home? Then her mind started racing as she thought of something. "How did you know Shanell's name? I've never mentioned her name to you and I only told you I was bringing someone, but I didn't say who."

"Yes, I know. To be honest with you, I researched you after getting that sexy message. I had to see who this was sending me such a message.

In my position, I have to be careful of those type of situations. I hope this doesn't deter you from us."

Candy stared at him with no response. She didn't know how she should be feeling after learning all of this. It was too much and too fast for her. A part of her was doing backflips learning his identity. But another part of her wished they were still at the sexting each other without their, well, his identity being known. She was beginning to feel like this was a mistake coming there and turned to leave.

"Wait, Candice. Please, don't go," Verdell said. He sounded panicky. There was no way he was going to let her get away. He was into this woman, not just because of their racy texts, but from those where they talked about any and everything for hours on end. Along with reading her positive posts on her social media pages, watching her YouTube channel, he knew she was someone he wanted to be in the presence of. Her spirit was genuine. He could feel that even now, when she wanted to run away. "I'm sorry if my confession makes you uncomfortable. Please believe me, I wasn't, and I am not trying to deceive you. I just have to be careful. People are always trying to find some way to get close to me so they can try and get whatever the can from me. I don't nor I have ever thought this was the case with you."

"Why me? You can have any woman you want. So, what about me has you texting me all day every day for the past four months?" Candy asked in a shaky voice.

"Everything I learned about you. From our texts, to your social media pages, everything I've learned about you along with how beautiful you are is why you. Yes, I can have whatever woman I want, and I want

141

you," he was now standing so close to her that she could feel his breath on her when he spoke.

"I'm not sure I'd be a good fit in your world. I'm an around the way girl, straight from the hood. You, you're from the upper echelon. You grew up having the best of everything. I had to take the hand-me-downs from my sisters as we grew. So, Mr. Mcintosh, I'm not so sure we'd be good for each other. I'm not looking for a right now thing. I'm looking for my forever."

"And you don't think I already know everything you just said? I did a full background check on you before I replied to your text. I know where you're from and I know where I'm from. But where we're from has no effect on the right now. You can't stand here and tell me that you don't have feelings for me, that the past four months don't mean anything to you. I want you, Candice Larae Carson, around the way girl and all that comes with you."

He didn't let her say another word. He leaned down and kissed her before she could utter a word. He pulled her to his body and held her tightly as he kissed her, sucking on her tongue gently then rough. He had to shut her mind off so she can let this thing flow. Candy melted in his embrace. She dropped her purse on the floor and wrapped her arms around his neck. She stood on her tip toes to meet his kisses. They sucked and nibbled on each other tongues and lips. When they came up for air, Candy was ready for more than a kiss. She was ready to feel that steel between his legs that was pressing against her belly.

"Aah, aah, aah!" Shanell's voice can be heard screaming from one of the nearby rooms. Verdell and Candy stared at each other before bursting out in laughter.

"Well, we see they are getting to know each other very well," Verdell said.

"Yep, sounds like it," Candy replied. "Now can we go and do the same?"

"Oh, so eager now, aren't we?" Verdell joked.

"Very," Candy winked.

Verdell bent down and picked up her purse. He grabbed her hand and led her out of the dining room and down the hall. They passed the room Shanell and Bradford was in and could hear their grunts and moans very much so now. Candy couldn't tell who was putting it down on who because they both were moaning as if they were having the best sex of their lives. But their moans were making Candy just as horny and she was so ready to be calling out the same way.

She couldn't wait until they were in his bedroom. Candy tugged on his hand and stopped him halfway up the stairs. He turned to look at her and she pulled him down to her level. She fondled with his sweatpants, pulling them along with his boxers down to his ankles. She cooed at the site of his dick poking at her as if to say, 'I'm all yours.' She licked her lips then spat on the tip before sucking him into her mouth. "Mmm," Verdell moaned as he watched her deep throat all ten inches of him.

She took him to the back of her throat and swallowed. "Sss, mmm," Verdell moaned out again. Candy swallowed a couple more times. She took him out of her mouth and ran her tongue along the long vein that strained out. With one hand she massaged his balls as she bobbed up and down on his shaft. She moaned when she tasted his precum. He tasted of cinnamon and it was turning her on so much that she reached between her legs and slid her fingers through the side of her thong and began playing with her clit.

"Candy, you're going to make me come," Verdell said. Watching her play with her pussy while giving him head was the sexiest thing he ever saw. When she took him to the back of her mouth again then swallowed and moaned, he exploded in her mouth, squirting his seed down her throat. Candy swallowed it all without gagging. Him coming in her mouth cause her to have an orgasm behind him.

When she pulled him out of her mouth, Verdell had to take a seat on one of the steps because his legs felt like noodles from her head game. She was still playing with her pussy, rubbing her nectar around her clit and pussy lips. She stood then pulled her thong off. She then pulled her dress off followed by her bra.

1. Candy stood before Verdell naked and vulnerable. She wasn't in the best shape. She had a small pudge from when she was overweight. At one point she was over two hundred pounds but within the past year she'd lost over fifty pounds. She went from a size sixteen down to a size twelve. She made sure that she rubbed coco butter on her body every day to keep the cellulite down to a minimum and only had three that just wouldn't go away. But Verdell didn't care about any of that. She was the most

beautiful woman in his eyes and seeing her naked had him rock hard in record time.

"Come here and sit that pretty pussy on my face," he pulled her to him as he leaned back on the stairs. She straddled his face and moaned as soon as his tongue made contact with her sensitive clit. She wrapped her hand around the railing and rode his face. He expertly lapped her honey as it oozed out of her honey cone. He had one hand on an ass cheek while the other stroked his dick. Verdell literally was putting his mark on Candy's pussy as he spelled out his entire name on it.

"Ooh shit, yes Ver-uh-dell," Candy called out. He only got to the 'E' in Verdell when she began coming on his tongue. "Aah, yes!" Candy rode his face faster, smearing all her juices over his face. That didn't stop him from continuing to fuck her with his tongue. He refused to stop until he spelled out his full name on her pussy. By the time he got the last letter in his last name, Candy had come two more times.

Verdell tapped her butt cheek and she lifted up off his face. Candy slid down and positioned her pussy at the head of his dick. She plopped down as he pumped up into her. "Uuh," they both said. Right on the steps, Verdell and Candy fucked each other hard. She rode him fast and hard in a rowing method, moving back and forth as he pumped up in and out of her with that same intense. Verdell latched on to one of her nipples and sucked on it. Having her breast suckled on always drove Candy crazy and the way Verdell was latched on had her fourth orgasm taking over.

"Damn, Candy! Ride this dick, baby! Fuck this dick!" Verdell said. His toes curled in his sneakers as she rode his dick faster and harder. He felt her legs shaking as came long and hard on his dick. Her muscles clamped down on him and he damn near exploded too, but he held out. He didn't want to come just yet. He waited until her legs stopped shaking before he lifter her off him and got behind her.

"Here, put your knees on this so you won't get rug burn." Verdell pulled his t-shirt off and Candy put it on the step.

As soon as she was situated, he plunged in her from behind then pulled out. "Aaah!" Candy cried out. She wondered if this position was what had Shanell screaming out like this. Verdell repeated the process a couple more times that dug off in her pussy with quick but long strokes that hit her spot from every angle. "Oh god. I'm about to come again," Candy called out.

Verdell smacked Candy's ass and she lost it. Her legs shook faster than earlier. Her walls sucked Verdell's dick in and latched on as she came. His dick had become a prisoner inside her cove and wouldn't be free until she came down from her sexual high. He was just fine with that as he continued to thrust in her as he felt his nut coming up.

"Squeeze harder on this dick. Make it yours, baby," Verdell said as he thrust harder in her. Candy squeezed her muscles harder around him and sucked him in further. "Shit, baby! Oh, Candice, I'm about to come in this pussy!" Verdell released in her what felt like buckets of his semen. Just like Candy did with her mouth when he came down her throat, her pussy sucked in all he released.

Verdell fell over on her and rain kisses on the side of her face. They both were spent. Their bodies were dripped in sweat. They lay with him on top and still inside her as they tried to getting their breathing under control. "That was great!" Candy admitted.

"That was miraculous," Verdell countered.

"It was a spectacular show, too," Shanell called up to them.

Candy and Verdell looked down to see Shanell bent over the table that sat smack in the center of the foyer with Brad behind her hitting it from the back. They were on their way to his room when they were halted by Verdell and Candy getting their freak on, on the stairs. Watching them having sex turned Shanell on and she turned to Brad and began giving him a hand job to get him erect. It didn't take long for him since he was wishing it was him Candy was riding instead of his brother. She reminded him of one of his favorite porn stars by how she was bouncing her bootylicious ass. He bent Shanell over on the table and entered her.

"Well damn," Verdell said as he and Candy were now viewers of a live porn flick. They watched as Brad placed one of Shanell's legs on the table and rode her fast. Shanell held on to the edge of the table tossing her ass back on him.

Candy could feel Verdell growing hard inside her and she squeezed her muscles around him. "Mmm, you ready for another round, too?" Verdell asked as he slowly moved in and out of her.

"Yes, but can we go on up to your room?" Candy said not taking her eyes off her friend and Brad.

"Yes, but I want you to come on my dick first. That shit feels so damn good," Verdell moaned her ear. He pumped harder and before you

147

know it, there were nothing but moans and groans coming from both couples as they watched each other fuck to their next climaxes.

Shanell was the first to come followed by Candy. Just hearing Shanell's moans made Candy come but it was Verdell's thrusts on her g-spot that took her over the edge. She was pleasantly surprised at how he learned of her g-spot so quickly and knew just the right amount of friction to put there and on her clit at the same time to bring her to a mind-blowing orgasm. With both ladies crying out in unison making a beautiful ballad, both brothers released inside of their partners at the same time.

"Shit, Candy!"

"Fuck, Shanell!"

They all were done and couldn't believe they just had sex in front of each other that way. At the same time, they are were thinking how exotic it was. After several minutes of catching their breath, each couple ventured off to their respective rooms. Verdell and Candy took a long hot shower together that consisted of round three for them before they fell asleep in bed in each other's arms, while Brad and Shanell went several more rounds before they too fell asleep in each other's arms.

The next morning, Verdell woke Candy up by way of his face buried between her legs. Down in Brad's room, he and Shanell were in the shower getting their morning fix of sexual lust. By eight a.m., both couples had fucked and sucked their way to several climaxes before they dressed for the day. Candy and Shanell put back on the clothes they'd worn over the night before while the men were in their power suits. They met in the dining room where they all had breakfast together and made small talk. Once they were done eating, the men escorted them to Candy's car and kissed them goodbye, promising to see each other later.

"Bitch, I'm so glad your ass sent that sext message to the wrong damn number!" Shanell exclaimed.

"Who you telling? Girl, me too!" Candy shook her head. Her pussy pulsated just thinking about last night's events.

"That was the best sex I ever had!" Shanell ranted. "And who'd thought you had some freak in you? Yeah I saw you checking me and Brad out."

"What did you expect? Shit y'all were butt ass naked on the damn table getting it on! Hell yeah, I was looking, and that shit turned me on! You know I never was into porn flicks but watching y'all did something to me. But then again, I did have a big dick that was still inside my pussy at the time. Hell, I'm with you on that best sex ever. Verdell fucked me better than any other guy I've been with and I'm not afraid to say he got a bitch hooked!" Candy ranted and raved.

Both ladies laughed and discussed their night on the way home. Candy had just pulled up at Shanell's house when both of their phones chimed. They looked at each other, then their phones.

Verdell: Hey beautiful. I had a great time last night and this morning.

Candy: Hey handsome. So, did I

Verdell: Can I see u 2nite?

Candy: Of course…what time?

Verdell: I'll pick u up at 7:30. I placed a little something in your purse...

Verdell: go get something nice to wear to a gala function, but don't wear panties

Candy: Oh wow! Thnx babe and don't worry, I'm gonna be classy and sexy for ya muah!

Verdell: I can't wait to see u

Brad: Hey sexy...so glad u came with ur girl last night...wasn't expecting that

Shanell: Hey urself....so glad I came as well...wasn't expecting any of that either

Brad: I wanna see where we can take this...you down or was it just a fun nite 4 u

Shanell: Oh, I'm down.... funny how the wrong number turned out to be the right number

Brad: ikr....so I want u to go to this gala with me tonight...u down

Shanell: Sure

Brad: b at your girl's spot....my bro and I will pick y'all up there.

Shanell: aight

Brad: I'm gonna have a courier bring u something.... go get a sexy as dress for tonight

Shanell: Well alright then!

Shanell: I'm gonna b so sexy u just might want to give another live performance

Brad: lol I'll c u 2nite sexy

Shanell: indeed handsome

"Candy, we have officially arrived, thanks to your wrong number ass!" Shanell joked.

The ladies hugged and Candy pulled off on her way home for some much-needed sleep. As she drove, she thanked her spiritual maker for crossing her path with Verdell's. She didn't know if what they had would last long, but this time around she decided not to worry about the what ifs and just live in the moment. Shit had she not sexted the wrong number, she would not have gotten sexed the way she did last night and this morning.

Chapter 12: The Subway

I stood off to the side of the crowd as we all waited for the train to pull up at the station. It was six p.m. and it was the evening crowd heading home after a long day's work. I had my headphones on blast listening to Tupac so no one would try and hold a conversation with me. However, when I saw this brother rushing down the steps wearing a pair of coveralls and some Timbs, I was more than willing to turn down the volume on my music to spark up a convo with him.

His foot hit the last step when the train came pulling up. I purposefully made a b-line in his direction so I could get up close and personal to him. We shoved ours way through the door before it would close. We were packed like sardines; it was so crowded, but I ended up sandwiched between ole boy and overweight guy who looked like he was on his last bit of energy.

I smiled when I felt his hand grab ahold of my waist. He pulled my backside closer to his front and I could feel his bulge against my ass. "I saw you checking me out, ma. You like what you see?" he pulled my headphones aside and whispered in my ear.

"Yeah, I was and yeah I like what I see. That also means you checking me out to," I spoke so only he could hear me.

"I'm liking all of this. So is my man. You see you woke him up," he pushed his bulge more into my ass. I bit down on my lip at the feel of him. I slowly rolled my ass against him. Why the hell did I do that? My panties got soaked from the wetness of my juices trickling down onto them.

The train stopped at the next station. Several people got off, but even more got on pushing me further into him, squeezing us in a corner. I felt his hand on my thigh. He slowly moved it up and under my skirt. He moved my panties to the side and ran his fingers over my wet pussy. He bit down in the side of my neck and I gasped. "Shh," he whispered in my ear.

I felt his free hand moving between our bodies as he unzipped his coveralls. He continued to fondle between our bodies when I felt my skirt being pushed up from behind. I felt the tip of his dick at my backside. I stood on my tip toes so he could position the head at my opening. He rubbed the head between my pussy lips, coating it with my juices before sliding inside me. I let out a slight moan as we stood there connected, not moving, just enjoying the feel of each other. Hell, I was glad for that since I needed to adjust to his size.

At another stop, once again some people got off and others got on, yet we were still smushed in the corner. He began thrusting in me slowly. I wrapped my hand around the pole next to me and slightly bent over to take more of him in me. I bit down on my lip to suppress my moans as his thrusting was feeling good. Somehow, he was able to grab my left leg and hoist it up as he fucked me from behind. I was glad big boy was still in front of me because he blocked us from other nearby passengers.

Dude picked up the pace and I threw my pussy back on him matching his strokes. I whimpered at how amazing he was feeling. The adrenaline of being fucked in public where we could be caught at any given moment had me on a natural high. Never in my life had I imagined being fucked on the subway by a stranger. The thought alone had my orgasm building.

"I need you to come for me, ma," dude bent over and whispered in my ear. We were nearing the next stop, which was my stop and I wanted to come just as well. I positioned his hand that was lingering on my mound onto my clit. He took that as his cue and began rubbing my pearl and thrusting faster inside of me. I bit down so hard on my bottom lip to suppress my moans; I drew blood.

"Ma, we almost at my stop. Do your thang so I can get mine," he demanded and just like that I was coming.

"Mmm, ooh," I let out not able to hold my moans in any longer. I came hard on his dick. My walls clamped down on his dick and he grunted as he began to come as well. We were pulling up to our stop when he pulled out of me. He pulled my skirt back down over my ass and I could feel him positioning his dick back inside his coveralls before zipping it up.

"You take this train every day?" he asked me.

"Monday through Friday for work. And you?"

"Same here. I'm looking forward to meeting you here tomorrow," he said.

"Likewise. Same bat time, same bat station." We both laughed.

The train came to a stop and we pushed our way through the crowd to exit. We climbed the steps leading to the streets, never saying a word as we went in opposite directions. I turned my headphones back up and bobbed my head to the music as I made my way home. As I walked the three blocks home, I ran the entire event through my head piecing together an outfit, thinking of something for easy access.

The next day, I was the one rushing down the steps in hopes of not missing the train. A meeting I had ran over. I had to high tail it to get to the station in time. Luckily, I did and slid right on over to where Mr. Coveralls was, in the corner. I squeezed my way right in between him and an Asian couple. Unfortunately, they were not big and tall as the guy from yesterday, so we were limited on any type of action. This didn't deter him from moving his fingers inside me and fingering me to an orgasm. To say I was disappointed I wouldn't be able to feel his rod inside of me was an understatement. "Don't worry, ma. There's always tomorrow," he whispered in my ear as the train came to a halt at our stop.

Afterward, I rushed home. His fingers felt great, but I needed, wanted more. As soon as I was home, I raced to my bedroom and pulled out my trusted B.O.B., battery operated boyfriend. I turned the vibration up to the highest notch then placed him inside my wet canal. I fucked that dildo to a mind-blowing orgasm, fantasizing of my subway lover. That night I went to bed with dreams of him and hopes the next day I'd get my fix.

I was sad I didn't see him on the train the next day. I wondered what could have happened to him. I went home and had to get myself off again. I gave myself three orgasms with thoughts of him on my mind. I woke up the following morning with him on my mind and once again gave myself an orgasm before climbing out of bed and starting my day.

Somehow, I got to work ten minutes earlier than I normally do. I 'm glad I did since everyone seemed to be in a frenzy. It turned out we were getting a new department manager and from what the rumors were, he was a hard ass. Personally, I didn't understand why they were all running around like chickens with their heads cut off. If you're doing your job as you're supposed to then you had no worries. I mean, it's only common sense. Anyway, Mr. Curtland called a mandatory meeting at the beginning of the shift to introduce us to the new department manager. When I tell you, my mouth dropped and my pussy synched when my eyes fell on the man who I was to now call my boss.

Of all people in the world, how that hell did it end being my subway lover? To say I was embarrassed! What made matters worse was that he acted as if we hadn't had an encounter with each other in any form. He didn't even look my way as he stood next to Mr. Curtland in the middle of the circle we were in.

"Ladies and gentlemen let me introduce you to Aaron Davis, your new department manager. Mr. Davis comes from our Charlotte office and was promoted to this position after working under Jenna Franklin. Let's all give him a warm welcome."

Everyone clapped and sounded off with their welcomes. I did neither. All I wanted to do was get the hell out of there. I had no well greetings for him, Mr. Davis. I eased my way behind my homegirl, Renee. Since he hadn't looked my way, I had no problem of him missing me as he made his grand speech.

"Thank you all so much for the warm welcome. I look forward to us working together and bringing this department to the top of this region as well as within the company. I want to get to know each of you a bit better, so I'll be calling you in to my office one by one so we can chat a bit. This will also give me a chance to see where you are and what we can do with your skills to help each of you advance to the next level. Now, I've heard the rumors that I'm a hard ass. I assure you that's not true. I am by the book, but I also want us all to succeed. So, the rumors that you've heard came from those who didn't want to follow the book or to succeed. I hope that won't be the case here."

Mr. Davis looked around to everyone and our eyes met when Renee stepped to the side bringing me into view. I cursed her under my breath because I knew she did that shit on purpose. Renee had no idea that Mr. Davis and I had our encounters. She knows, though, how shy I am around new people and had been trying to get me out of my shell as of lately. However, she was totally clueless as to how out of my shell he had me. I saw the smirk he made before tearing his eyes away and turning to face my other coworkers.

"I think the best way to start would be by going down the list alphabetically. So, Ryan, send in the first person and let's all get back to work. Have a great day," Mr. Davis said. He said something to Mr. Curtland that only he could hear then walked away.

We all broke out and headed back to our cubicles. Several comments of how fine the new director was or how they felt he was going to be firing people as they heard were being discussed. I plopped down in my seat and thanked God my name was the very last on the list. That was something I hated, but right now I could do a cartwheel with excitement. "So, what do you think of our new DM?" Renee came and sat on the edge of my desk.

"I don't think anything," I shrugged.

"Seriously, Zoe. Don't you think he's hot? I mean, that man can get it." Renee bit down on her lip and made a seductive face. I broke out laughing at her. She could be so inappropriate at times.

"Do you really need to be making that face?" I half-joked.

"Oh, come on, Zoe. Loosen up! Get out of that bubble of yours and let loose sometime. Damn!"

"Why are you getting so upset, Renee? Just because I refuse to let my freak flag fly for the world to see is not a reason."

"I'm sorry, okay? But you don't do anything except go to work and back home. When was the last time you stepped outside your bubble and did something spontaneous?"

"Well—" I said but was cut off when Leon walked over.

"Hey Renee, Mr. Davis is asking for you," he told her.

Thank you! I wasn't a good liar and didn't know how I would be able to tell her my subway rendezvous without mentioning it was our new manager. Renee stood and left without another word or glance my way. I know she's upset with me, but she'll be okay. I'm used to her temper tantrums, so I do as I always do and ignore them.

The day went on as more of my coworkers were called in to meet with Mr. Davis. I busied myself working on a coupled of projects assigned to me. During lunch, several conversations of what they met with him about floated throughout the break room. Some were chill while others were not so chill. It seems Mr. Davis had done his homework prior to today and these meetings were actually evaluations. I chuckled as I listened to them bitching about him telling them the same thing Willona and Mr. Curtland had been telling them for quite some time. Do your job and you won't have any problems. The very people bitching were the ones who came to work late, half assed work, and left early or just didn't come to work.

I had fifteen minutes before my workday ended and my weekend was to start. After much begging and pleading from Renee, I finally agreed to hang out with her tonight for happy hour. I'm not big on drinking and why I never went with her, but I figured I'd have a glass of wine and something to eat just to make her happy. I was packing up and shutting down my computer when Mr. Curtland came up to me.

"Zoe, Mr. Davis wants to see you now."

"Are you serious? Now? When it's time to go?" I was vexed. What nerve of him to call me in when it's quitting time.

"Yes, yes, and yes. Go on. Don't keep the man waiting." Mr. Curtland walked off without another word.

"Hey, Renee. You go on ahead. I have to go see Mr. Davis. I'll chat up to you," I stopped at her desk and relayed the news to her.

"He still wants to see you even though you're off the clock? That's bullshit!" Renee fussed.

"It is but if I want to keep my job, then I have to go see him now," I told her.

"Well, okay. But still come out, Zoe. I want you to have some fun for once in a while." Renee hugged me.

We walked to the elevators together. She pressed the down button while I pressed the up button. We waved bye to each other when the elevator opened for me. I hopped on and pressed the button to the twelfth floor. On the ride up, I smoothed my dress and fixed my hair looking at my reflection in the polished door. I wouldn't say I was a beauty queen, but I know I'm not an ugly duckling. I guess you can say I'm average looking. I'm five foot four, a hundred and twenty-five pounds, caramel complexion. I have brown doe eyes, a wide nose, and full lips. My hair is shoulder length with no real style to it. Today it's pulled to the back in a ponytail. I don't wear makeup except for eyeliner and clear lip gloss.

When the elevator doors opened, I slowly eased off and followed the glass wall around that led to the director's office. I was always in awe when I came up here. The view of the city was beautiful. It was just picture perfect. I stopped in front of the closed door and read the sparkling new name plate. Aaron Davis shined brightly on the brass plate. I let out a breath, then knocked on the door.

"Come in," he said. I turned the knob and opened the door. I stepped inside and looked around the office. It looked much differently than how Willona had it decorated. It was more modern and brighter than the last time I was there. He even replaced the old window blinds with some new shades that blocked out the light. "Close the door and have a seat, Miss Zellwig," he instructed not looking up from his computer.

I did as instructed and took a seat in one of the leather chairs situated in front of his desk placing my bag in the other seat. I crossed my legs and that seemed to catch his attention. His eyes roamed over my legs and he licked his lips. His eyes continued to roam over my body until they landed on my eyes. He sat looking at me as if he was in a trance. I gave him that same stare, not blinking, not moving, hell not breathing; just waiting for him to make the first move. His office phone ringing broke our gaze. I exhaled as he picked up the phone.

"Hello," he said while watching me. He listened to the person on the other end for a few moments before finally saying, "No, you can go on home. Miss Zellwig is in good hands," he had the nerve to wink when he said that. I had the nerve to be turned on. "Alright. You have a good weekend as well." Mr. Davis hung up the phone.

"Sorry about that. Shall we get down to the matter at hand?" Mr. Davis asked me.

"I'd like that since I'm off the clock and not getting paid overtime," I replied.

"Okay then. I've looked over your file and since you've been here you've done some great work. You don't have any infractions and I've heard nothing but good things about you. So, tell me, Miss Zellwig, why aren't you in a managerial position?"

I thought about his question before answering. It really wasn't what I thought he was going to ask though. Honestly, I didn't know what he wanted to talk about. But I let my mind ponder his question. "Well, I never thought about it to be honest." That was all I could come up with.

"Really? Why do you think that? I ask because your portfolio and ads are great. You work well alone as with others based on the others. When I asked if they could choose someone to work on a project with, rather it be a last-minute thing, or one that had an extended deadline, they all mentioned you. As long as I've been in upper management, never have I had an entire team to name only one person they'd choose. When I ask them why, they say you're honest, helpful, and hold your own. You don't let them get over on you, even when they've tried. But more importantly you don't belittle them. I would say these are the makings of a great manager. Wouldn't you?"

I was in total awe at the things said by my coworkers. I never knew they felt that way. I mean, I come to work, do my job, and go home. I don't seek any accolades from anybody. I just do my job. But I can admit that it's great to know they look up to me that way. It's nice to know my hard work has paid off. "I'm shocked they all think so highly of me. I never knew that. I guess I never thought about management because it was never presented to me until now. I'm not opposed to it if a position was to become available."

"That's good to hear because there will be a position open within the next few weeks. Ryan has been promoted and will be leaving this office. We need to fill his slot and these interviews today were to see who was best qualified within this department. With you're A-1 file and the rave reviews from your peers, I see no reason you shouldn't be the one to take his place."

"Wow, that's, that's great news! Thank you so much!" This day couldn't get any better. I just got a promotion! Yay for me!

"Now that we have that out of the way, we have another matter to discuss." Mr. Davis licked his lips. His eyes turned dark and bore into me. My nipples hardened and my clit began throbbing.

"Um, yeah we do. Did you know I worked here when we... you know?"

"Honestly, yes. I saw you when I came in on Tuesday. But I wasn't expecting for us to you know, on the subway."

"I wasn't expecting that at all. That's definitely not something I have ever done in my life. Renee has been telling me I needed to be spontaneous and step outside my shy box, and the one or two times I did, it turns out to be with my now new boss."

"It was truly spontaneous for me, too. I've never done something like that in a very public place. I took a chance and went for it."

"And I accepted with no regards."

"Was it good to you? It was to me."

"Yes, yes it was," I said breathlessly. I had to uncross then cross my legs again to try and soothe my throbbing clit. It wasn't helping.

"I've thought about you every day since then."

"I've thought about you as well."

"So, Miss Zellwig, how do you suppose we handle this moving forward?" Mr. Davis stood and moved around the desk and took a seat on the edge of the desk next to my seat. All of a sudden, the heat turned up several notches and I felt sweat bubbles popping up on my forehead.

"I'm new to this so you should come up with a few suggestions. But can you call me Zoe? I'm not old so no need for the formalities especially after what we did."

"I agree and you can call me Aaron."

"Okay, Aaron."

"I want to kiss you, Zoe. Can I kiss you?"

"Yes."

He took my hand and pulled me up to him. I stood between his legs and we began to kiss. His hands grabbed my ass, which wasn't all that big but just enough, and squeezed my cheeks. He pulled my dress up over my ass and rubbed my bare ass cheeks before grabbing a hold of my thong and tearing the thin fabric off. I undid his tie and unbuttoned his shirt. He unzipped my dress and we undressed. "What if someone comes in?" I asked even though it was a bit too late to ask since I was standing in nothing but my bra and heels.

"I made sure you were my last for the night so everyone would be gone. I knew I wouldn't be able to meet with you and not want to touch you," he told me as he locked the door.

For the strangest reason, with Aaron I let all my inhibitions go and let my shyness dim. I undid my bra and let it fall to the floor. I sat on the desk Aaron was just sitting at and placed my foot on the chair next to me. I motioned with the curl of my finger for him to come to me. I was feeling my sexual beast moving to the forefront and wanted to let everything go.

Aaron removed his shoes, pants and boxers then slowly came toward me. I placed a hand on my mound and began playing with my clit. This stopped Aaron's movement toward me and for several minutes he stroked himself as he watched me masturbate. This turned me on more and I began to come all over my fingers. I licked my lips when I saw precum oozing out the tip of his dick. I pulled my fingers out of my lover nest and licked my juices off them and moaned in pleasure.

"Damn, girl, I need a taste if you're moaning like that," Aaron said taking two steps and was in front of me. I smiled and placed a hand on top of his head to lower him down to my juicy peach. He got on his knees and dove into my pussy, tongue first. He lapped up the remnants of my orgasm around the folds and licking my inner thighs. When he inserted his tongue inside my pussy, I threw my head back in pleasure. I scooted my ass closer to the edge of the desk while pushing his face deeper into my pussy.

I gyrated my pelvis in line with his tongue, bringing on a second orgasm. I spread my legs further apart and fucked his tongue, riding it as my orgasm flushed through my body. "Aah, yes! Suck this pussy!" My legs shook as I came hard in his mouth. I tugged on my nipples intensifying my orgasm even more.

Aaron licked my kitty a few more minutes. When he pulled away and stood, I hopped off the desk and pushed him into the chair. I got squatted between his legs and took him into my mouth. Licking the precum that was already coating the tip, I slurped it up tasting the salty fluid mixing it with my saliva. I bobbed my head up and down his shaft, taking him to the back of my throat. I gagged a bit since he was on the big size. To be honest had I actually seen how big he was before did the do on the subway, I probably wouldn't have fucked him, and I definitely wouldn't be sucking him now.

I must have been doing my thing because Aaron began moaning and he grabbed my hair when I twirled my tongue along the shaft. I pulled him out with a pop then placed him back in my mouth. I sucked on the head while massaging his balls. "Ooh, Zoe. Shit, girl!" I sucked him until he came down my throat. I swallowed every drop bringing myself another orgasm being that I was masturbating as I gave him head. I continued to suck Aaron until he was hard again.

I stood and climbed onto his lap. We shared another kiss as I slid down his shaft. Once I was completely filled by him, I began to ride him. I bounced up and down on him fast and hard. "Feels so good," I said.

I twerked my pussy on him finding my g-spot. Aaron thrust up as I came down and it was like someone pushing the button signaling for the elevator to come to their floor. He kept hitting my spot repeatedly. I was panting like I was running a marathon, as yet another orgasm shot through me. "Oh shit! Fuck me!"

Aaron gripped my ass and stood, bouncing up and down on his dick. He laid me on the desk and placed my legs on his shoulders. He began to beat my pussy into a pulp as he fucks me fast and hard. All I could do was hold on to the edges of the desk and enjoy the ride of my life. My breast bounced up and down in rhythm with Aaron's thrusts. I met his strokes as he found my spot again and hit it again repeatedly. "Aaron, I'm coming again! Oh baby!"

"Mmm hmm, let that shit go, ma."

I couldn't even begin to tell you what the hell I yelled out because my words were blended in together but got caught in my throat as I skeeted on his dick and down his legs. I felt my juices raining down onto the desk underneath me. My eyes rolled to the back of my head and I felt like I was on the verge of passing out. Y'all I think I in over on my head with this one. I mean, this dick is so good, I'm seeing stars and shit. Ladies, have you ever had dick that damn good? Someone please help a sista out! I cannot ever remember having these many orgasms in one day, and oh my word I'm loving every last one of them!

"Sss, mmm, Zoe. I'm about to come in this pussy," I hear Aaron say just as he squirted his load inside me. He jerked a few times before he collapsed on top of me. We lie there on the desk getting our breathing back to normal.

Aaron finally stood and pulled out of me. My kitty contracted a few times like aftershocks from an earthquake. My body tingled at the emptiness I felt when he disconnected from me. The void I was feeling was that same feeling I had a couple of days ago when all he was able to give me were his fingers. I wanted more of him and having his dick inside me made me feel complete. But how could this be? How could I feel complete with him inside me when we just met? It just wasn't making sense to me at all.

I sat up and watched him as he gathered his clothes. His back remained to me the entire time he got dressed. The emptiness I was feeling soon disappeared and I then felt like a damn fool. Who was I fooling thinking our subway rendezvous would morph into something more? What would make me even think such a thing? I got played. He said what needed to be said to get the ass one last time. And you know what? As much as I want to be mad, I'm not. I'm glad we got in this last rumble especially since I'm up for this promotion. Knowing that, we wouldn't be able to get down like this anymore anyway. I never did mix my professional life with my personal life, so this last go was what I needed to get him out of my system.

"How about we take this back to my place? Or yours? Whichever you prefer," Aaron said to me.

"Huh? I'm sorry. What did you say?" I shook my head in confusion. What the hell?

"I asked if we could take this back to my place or yours."

"Oh, um, well, I um," I couldn't form any words at the moment because I didn't know what to say.

"Zoe, are you okay?"

"Yeah, I'm good. I guess, I wasn't expecting you to want to take this any further than tonight since you spoke of me being promoted."

"Oh. I see. Is that what you want?"

"No, no. I just; I don't know. I thought after tonight that would be it for us," I ran a hand through my hair. "You seemed disconnected from me after you pulled away and it made me feel uncomfortable," I breathe a sigh of relief. I got out what it was I really wanted to say.

Aaron stood there with a blank expression. He then frowned after analyzing my words then he looked confused. I could tell he was pondering what he wanted to say, making sure he had the correct words in place before he spoke. I'm sure I would have if I were in his shoes. Not understanding myself has been one of my very own issues, so I know he's having trouble right now.

"Zoe, I was just putting my clothes back on so we can leave before the cleaning personnel comes around. If I made you feel uncomfortable or insecure in any way, it wasn't my intentions, ma. I want to get to know this shy with some freak in her, smart, and beautiful woman is by the name of Zoe Zellwig." Aaron walked over to me. I was now fully dressed minus my ripped thong. He reached behind me and zipped my dress up. He then held on to my waist as he planted a soft kiss on my lips.

It made me feel good to hear him say those words to me. I didn't think Aaron would take me seriously after he sexed me on the subway before we even knew each other's names. Then to find out we would be working together. By the way, a thought ran across my mind. "Question, why were you wearing coveralls both days I saw you on the subway?"

"Oh that? Well I went to help my uncle at his auto shop. He was a man short those days. My cousin and his wife just had a baby so I filled in so he could help his wife and the new baby get settled in."

"That was thoughtful of you," I kissed his chin.

"That's just what family does. But enough about that. Can we go and see if we can get in a quickie on the train on our way to your place?" Aaron asked as he pumped his pelvis to mine.

"Only if you give me the D. I'm not wearing any panties, so I don't want no fingers this time around."

"Oh, I see I done started some shit with you. Let me find out you a freaky freak," Aaron teased as we left out of his office.

"You didn't know? Every woman has some freak in her. It just takes the right man to bring it out of her," I winked and sashayed ahead of him making my way towards the elevator. "Now come on and let's hurry so you can get me my fix in our favorite spot on the subway."

Part 3: Sizzling

Chapter 13: Masquerade Ball

Masquerade Ball

Date: October 26, 2019

Time: 8:00 p.m. – Until You Can No Longer Cum

You're cordially invited to a night of exploring your wildest dreams, living out your fantasies, and letting of all your inhibitions

This night is all about freeing your mind and giving in to your body's sexual desires

Requirements: This invitation, a mask and costume to describe your sexual alter ego, and the password that will be sent out to you via text message an hour before the event time.

I sat at my desk in my office reading my invitation over and over. A courier delivered it to me. The presentation was gorgeous! The box it came in was black velvet with a gold lock and key. When I opened it up, the inside was gold velvet. The invitation laid in the center of the box on display. I pulled it out and the front of it was of a golden gate with a fancy design like one you'd see at the entrance of an extravagant house. The background of the card was black velvet with the writing in gold calligraphy. This was the prettiest and most expensive invitation I'd ever seen.

I'd heard stories of this masquerade ball for years, but never in my life did I expect to get an actual invitation. I had all kinds of emotions running through me. I was happy to get an invite being this would be my first attendance. I was excited and nervous to see what would happen while there. Would I participate any anything or just watch? I had no clue at the time. All I knew was I needed to find the perfect mask and costume.

Instead of going online or going to a costume shop, I reached out to a local designer to see if we could come up with the perfect, custom made costume to reflect my sexual alter ego. Lucky for me, I was able to get an appointment for the very next day. I had a problem though. I didn't know who my sexual alter ego was. I didn't think I had one to be honest. I mean I'm not a virgin, but I've never done anything kinky. I've only had what they call vanilla type sex. You know, the usual positions like, missionary, doggy style, riding; I've never done anything over the top and I'm interested in seeing how this masquerade ball is going to open me up, literally and figuratively.

The next day, I met with Francois Belvedere, a local clothing designer I found online. His website had several pieces that I think would work for this type of event and hoped we could come up with something for me. When I arrived at his boutique, I was skeptical because the building looked abandoned. For a second I wasn't sure if I had the correct address but after looking over the information, I wrote down from our phone call, I was at the right place.

I had to ring the doorbell and wait for someone to come open up for me. A tall brunette with a pale face, big green eyes, and long black hair greeted me. She wore black eyeliner and piercings in her nose and lips. She was dressed in that gothic style with a black sheer top showing off a black bustier underneath, a black pleather skirt, fishnet stockings, and knee-length black boots. She was a gorgeous woman. In all honesty, I wanted to turn back around and get the hell away from there, but I sucked it up and stepped inside.

I was pleasantly surprised once I was inside. The décor was totally opposite of goth girl with very bright colors of white, pastel pink and blush tones. It looked more like a woman's closet with antique furnishings. There were displays of mannequins with some of the dresses I saw on the website and a few that were not.

"I'm Misty, Francois's assistant. He will be out in a few moments. While you wait, would you like something to drink?"

"Hi, Misty. It's nice to meet you. I'm Darcel Garrison and what do you have?"

"We have water, sodas, wine, champagne."

"I'll take a glass of white wine, please."

"Okay, you can have a seat on any of the lounge chairs while I get that wine for you."

"Thank you." I watched Misty disappear behind a white curtain. I walked around and got a closer look at a draped dress displayed on a mannequin. I touched the fabric and it felt soft, like satin. Some soft jazz music began playing all of a sudden, then Misty reappeared with a glass of wine and a tray of cheese and crackers. Behind her walked who I assumed was Francois.

Francois was a very pretty man. I can see him taking more time to get dressed than I would. I'm unsure if he's straight or gay though. He was dressed in a pair of skinny jeans and a long white flare shirt with puffy long sleeves. Like Misty, he had piercings in his lip, nose, and both ears. His face was clean shaven, youthful looking. He could actually be a model; he was just that handsome.

"Darcel, welcome to Belvedere. I am Francois Belvedere."

"It's a pleasure to meet you," I said taking a hold of his extended hand for a shake. His hand was so soft, but his handshake was firm.

"So, tell me, what is it that you're looking for. Misty said you need a costume and mask for a party."

"Yes, I need to come with a costume that reflects my personality, um, my alter ego to be exact. But the problem is, I don't know who or what my alter ego is," I bit down on my bottom lip. My throat became dry from nervousness. I gulped down the wine.

"I see. Well, let's sit and chat for a bit. I'm sure we can find a concept for you." Francois ushered me over to one of the chaise lounges.

I jumped when I felt a hand on my shoulder and run down my back. I turned to see Misty standing behind me with a smile on her face. "Would you like another glass of wine?"

"Oh, um, sure."

"So Darcel, tell me a little bit about you. What type of work do you do? What do you do for fun? What is your favorite color? These things will help me to figure out who your alter ego may be or could be," Francois said. He placed a hand on my thigh, and I got moist all of a sudden.

"Oh okay. Let's see. I own a consulting business. Going to a spa is what I do for fun and my favorite color is pink. I don't get out that much, so I don't really have any hobbies."

Misty returned with another glass of wine. I noticed that it was filled to the rim this time. As soon as I had it in my hand, I took another long gulp. My clit began throbbing all of a sudden. I was aroused and started to feel warm.

"It seems we need to do something to break you out of your shell, Darcel. That will be the only way we can get to know your alter ego, don't you think?" Francois asked. I felt his hand move a little further up my thigh. He squeezed softly and I gasped. "Misty is going to bring out a few pieces for you to try on and we will come up with something based off your likes from them, okay?"

"S-sure," I said. Chills ran down my body and back up. My pussy was pulsating at the feel of Francois' hand so close to her. I was so aroused and didn't know what to do. I tried to sit still to get through my appointment, but I wasn't sure if I'd be able to.

Misty came out dressed in nothing but a black bustier, matching thong, and stilettos. She was pushing a rack of dresses in different lengths and styles. Seeing her big breast pushed up in her face, slim waist, thick thighs, and ass for a white girl had me turned on. I licked my lips when she stood in front of me and her fat pussy was directly in my line of sight. My hand seemed to have a mind of its own when it flew out and rubbed the back of her thigh. It moved up to her ass cheek and rubbed the soft round flesh.

I couldn't take my eyes off her pussy print. My nipples hardened when a flash of me licking her essence ran through my mind. I gulped down the rest of my wine then sat the glass on the table next to me, my other hand still on Misty's ass. I felt Francois's hand on my mound and him beginning to play with my clit. His fingers began moving in and out of my pussy. I removed my hand from Misty's ass and grabbed a hold of the chaise lounge. I spread my legs open giving Francois more access. I threw my head back and arched my back grinding on his fingers.

I moaned when I felt a tongue on my clit. I opened my eyes I had no idea I'd even closed and looked down to see Misty's face buried between my legs. I came right then. I grabbed the back of her head and shoved her face deeper into my pussy trying to put my entire pussy down her throat as she licked and sucked on my pussy and clit. I felt the zipper of my dress being tugged down. Francois slid it down my arms and to my waist. He unsnapped my bra then pulled it off as well.

Misty continued to eat my pussy, slurping up my cream as I came for a second time. Damn she can eat some pussy! Francois came around and placed a knee on the chaise beside me. He was now naked and had his dick out in his hand. Boy was his dick pretty! It was a nice size, not too big, but definitely not small. It was just the right length and had the right amount of girth. I stuck my tongue out and licked the tip of the one-eyed monster. Yum!

I wrapped my hand around him and took him to the back of my throat. I sucked his dick as Misty ate my pussy. I found myself competing with her to see how many licks it would take to get to the center of the tootsie pop. The only sounds were slurps and moans; so arousing to my ears. Shit, if anyone had told me I'd be in the center of a threesome on that day, I'd have spat in their eyes as I yelled blasphemy.

I don't know what the hell Misty was doing, but her tongue rolled in a peculiar way and my third orgasm shot through me so fast I had to pull Francois's dick out of me to keep from biting down on him. "Oh shit!" I screamed out as my legs began to shake and I started to squirt down her throat. She latched onto my clit and flicked the tip of her tongue on it quickly as I continued to come. "Shit! Fuck!"

This woman was relentless with eating pussy! I have never had my pussy eaten this way by any man I've been with. I can now see how a woman could get turned out by another woman if she put in work the way Misty was doing. I have never been into women, at least not until then. Shit I almost forgot about Francois until he bent down and latched onto a nipple and sucked it into his mouth. This intensified my orgasm since having my nipples sucked on was one of my pleasure points. Seriously, who goes to a clothing boutique to shop for a dress and ends up having a threesome? This was surreal but I be damned if it didn't feel so fucking good.

Misty finally withdrew from between my legs and looked up at me. She had the most pleasant look on her face. It was like she had just finished all the food on her plate and was now full. She licked her lips getting the remnants of my juices off and that made me come again. Damn!

Francois pulled away from my nipple and smiled up at me. I returned that same smile. He laid back on the chaise and pulling me with him. I saw that he already had on a condom. I positioned him at my opening and slid down until I had all of him inside of me. Misty straddled Francois's face as she faced me. I rode his dick as she rode his face. We kissed, rubbed, and sucked each other's tongues and tits.

Misty pushed me back so that I was laying down with Francois's dick still in me. She still rode his face as she leaned down and latched on to my clit. Having my clit sucked with a dick inside my pussy felt so amazing and I had a bigger orgasm than the ones before. I could even feel Misty coming from the vibrations of her mouth on my clit. It was the most exhilarating experience of my life. Not too long afterwards, Francois busted his nut in the condom.

We all lay in position a few moments catching our breath. One thing I realized as we began peeling our bodies away from each other was that my dress was ruined and no way in hell could I walk out wearing it. From sweat and my juices, it was done and over with.

Misty disappeared again and returned several minutes later wearing a robe and held a couple of washcloths in her hand. She placed one between my legs and cleaned me off with it. It was hot, wet, and soapy, smelled of lilac. She handed the other to Francois and he cleaned himself off. He gave her the cloth and she disappeared again. When she came back, she handed us each a robe. I stood and let my ruined dress fall to the floor. I stepped out of it and put on the robe before sitting back down.

"Do you see anything on this rack that interest you for the party, Darcel?" Francois asked. He got down to business as if we hadn't just fucked five minutes ago. I was cool with that though.

I stood and walked over to the rack. I looked over the dresses and came across a beautiful cocktail dress with a bustier top made of pink and silver Swarovski crystals with a silver feather skirt. It was beautiful! Right then I knew my alter ego was a sexy peacock!

Peacocks symbolize rejuvenation and integrity, as well as being very graceful and possessing a royal demeanor. I know that may not seem the case being I'd just fucked total strangers. However, I've always been told how graceful I carried myself. Anyway, I think the saying being a lady in the streets and a freak in the sheets fit me well. Don't you think?

"I'll take this one," I told Francois.

"I think you made the perfect choice, Darcel. I'll make up a mask to match it for you. I'm sure you will be the Belle of the ball." Francois smiled at me then turned to Misty. "Misty will you get this wrapped up please?" Misty nodded her head and took the dress from me. "Now please allow me to give you something else to put on since there was a mishap with your dress. Follow me."

I followed Francois into another part of the boutique where there were racks of women's business attire. I looked through a few racks before deciding on a soft pink two-piece pants suit. I reached in my purse and pulled my wallet out. I was pulling out my credit card when he stopped me. "That won't be necessary," he told me. I looked at him in confusion.

"After today's events, you earned and deserve them. Your money won't do here. All I ask is that you be a returning customer."

"I can do that," I told him.

"Good. I'll deliver both dress and mask to you in time for the party. I just know you're going to look stunning!"

"Thank you so much for everything and I'll see you soon!" Francois and I hugged before I left.

A month later and it was the night of the masquerade ball. I spent all day getting my hair and nails done and getting waxed all over that needed maintenance. I was happy to learn my friend Celeste had gotten an invitation also. Since we were two single ladies, we decided to take a limo to the ball together.

Francois had come through with my dress and mask. Instead of the dress I saw in the boutique, he made me a new one. This dress was all pink with pink Swarovski crystals in the bustier and pink feathers with a split on the left leg. I was happy the pink wasn't that bright flamingo or Pepto-Bismol pink, but was a soft subtle pink. The mask, however, was a shade brighter with silver crystals outlining the mask and pink and silver feathers sitting on one side. I finished my dress off with pink stilettos with silver crystals, my silver clutch, a diamond choker, and matching earrings. I slapped on my diamond bangle. I was looking like a million bucks.

Celeste arrived in the limo at 7:30 just as I received the text with the password. The text also instructed not to give out the password to anyone as this password was specific to me and me only. When I climbed inside the limo, I couldn't believe the costume Celeste was wearing. She literally had on the entire Wonder Woman suit and a mask that looked like it came from the kids' section at Walmart. I had to wonder if her invitation read the same as mine or something different. I mean, did she understand that we were going to a ball and not an actual Halloween party?

We made small talk on our way there but drank a bottle and a half of Moet. I was feeling good by the time we arrived. Celeste, I believe was beyond feeling good and was just right out drunk. I had a feeling she wasn't going to last past the next hour before she's passed out somewhere. The limo pulled up to a mansion that sat far off from the road. The gate looked just like the gate on my invitation and I thought that was just the cutest thing. As he drove up the long driveway, I touched up my makeup and hair. And just as I thought, Celeste was fast asleep.

The driver came to a stop and the door was opened by the valet. I instructed the driver to take Celeste back home and that I would call him an hour before I'm ready to be picked up. I stepped out of the car and was in awe of the entrance. I was so in love with the grand columns and large statues of lions. I walked up the stairs to the double doors where a man dressed in a suit holding a clip board checked in everyone upon entrance. He took the invitations, checked our names off, and pointed us to where a woman wearing a red Venice carnival feather peacock party mask, a matching bralette, and heels stood at a podium. She spoke briefly to each guest before directing them up the grand staircase. I was confused at the questions she was asking the guests before me and was nervous when it was my turn to speak with her.

"Good evening. How are you?" she asked politely.

"Good evening. I'm well and yourself?"

"I'm fine. Thank you for asking. You know I really wish I was at a resort or on a beach somewhere. I'd really love to go to one the ones that um, what they call them? They're over in Peru or Brazil. Do you know what they call them?"

"Oh, you're talking about an exotic beach resort. I've been to Brazil and it was lovely."

"I'm sure it is. Maybe I'll make it there sometime soon. Take the stairs and the ballroom is on your left. Enjoy."

"Thank you and have a good night."

As I took the stairs it was then I realized she got me to give her my specific password which was exotic. Clever! I made my way to the ballroom and was in total awe of the array of people that swarmed around in beautiful, colorful masks and costumes. The ballroom itself was decorated in mardi gras style décor. A live band played on the stage. Servers dressed as sex workers walked around with trays of different beverages and an assortment of finger food. I grabbed a glass of wine and a couple of the hors d'oeuvres of cheese and crackers.

"Ladies and gentlemen, I'd like to thank you all for coming out tonight. I am, King, your host for the evening. This year is uniquely different from our past balls. This year we have only two new invitees to this annual masquerade ball. After careful consideration, I felt there was no need any more newbies besides these two. So even though you all know the rules of the game, I still need to give them out for our newbies and as a refresher for those of you who tends have a brief memory loss."

The man standing on the stage speaking was wearing an actual crown, a black phantom of the opera half-face mask with a golden glitter design. From what I could see of his visible face, he was handsome. He was caramel in complexion, with dark eyes, a wide but not too big nose, and kissable lips outlined with a goatee. He was tall and the black vintage medieval coat and matching pants detailed a very muscular body. If that wasn't enough, the twelve pack that was on full display since he wasn't wearing a shirt underneath his coat, showed that he was very much into his health. My girly parts became aroused by the sight of him.

"Number one, please remember the nondisclosure forms you all signed. We take our privacy very serious because we have something to lose if any details of this event were to go public. Number two, we must respect each other at all times. Number three, don't forget your safe words. For our newbies, these are words you will need to use should you not feel comfortable with any of the activities you may indulge in or if the pain may become too much. And number four, let go of your inhibitions, explore your sexuality, indulge in your fantasies, and have fun." A thunder of clapping erupted amongst us. "Let the games begin in five, four, three, two, one." King along with the crowd counted down.

While King was speaking the band began breaking down their instruments and a deejay was setting up. After the countdown, the deejay kicked it off with R. Kelly's 12 Play. I slowly walked around the ball room grabbing wine and hors d'oeuvres off the trays as servers passed by me. I watched as some couples made their way onto the dancefloor and began to slow dance.

Something in my peripheral caught my attention and I turned to see a couple up against the wall fucking. They were dressed as the Princess and the Frog characters and the Frog held his Princess up with her legs wrapped around his waist as they had sex. I choked off my wine as they had sex in the open while people stood by watching them. To top that off, a lady dressed as Cinderella was on her knees giving her Prince Charming some head.

"Are you enjoying the evening so far, Miss Garrison?" a man whispered in my ear scaring the shit out of me. I turned to face him, and it turned out to be King. Geesh! He was extremely tall over my five-foot frame, but I liked that. Up close I could tell he was in his late thirties, maybe early forties, yet he still looked youthful and was even more good looking.

"Um, well, being that I just got here, I can only say the live band was great and the deejay is doing his thing. As for anything else, um, I can't speak on right now," I ran a hand through my hair as I looked around us. I was so ecstatic to receive an invitation to this party but didn't really think too much about what this party was all about. From what I saw, it was an orgy! As soon as the countdown was zero, people began fucking where they stood. I guess I was expecting a bit more, something more intimate, sensual.

"I know this could be overwhelming being this is your first time. This," King waved his hand around, "this room usually has the turn up.

185

But you have to explore the rest of the mansion. Each room has a different theme and activities going on. They don't all have all of this. You don't have to do anything you don't want to do."

"Yeah, I think I'll walk around and see what else is going on, 'cause this is a bit too much for me right now. Maybe I haven't had enough to drink yet," I let out a nervous laugh.

"Maybe," he smirked. A server came walking by with some mixed cocktails and stopped next to us. King grabbed a red drink with an umbrella stuck in an orange wedge and handed it to me. "Here, drink this. I think it will help you loosen up. Go ahead and mingle. I'll check on you later." King leaned down and kissed my cheek then walked away.

I watched King mingle with other guests as I stood there sipping on my drink. It tasted like a burst of tropical fruit exploded in my mouth. Before I knew it, I had drunk it all up. I decided to go check out the other rooms as I searched for another one of those drinks. I walked out of the ballroom and decided to go to my right. The first room I stopped at I could hear moaning on the other side of the door. I cracked the door open to see what they were doing but the sound was coming from a porn flick playing on the flat screen hoisted on the wall. The blonde hair, blue-eyed woman was bent over on the side of a chair getting fucked from behind by a muscular, dark-skinned brother. Looking at the size of his dick and the way he was pounding her, I could see why she was screaming like a banshee.

I pushed the door open further to see if anyone was inside the room, but it was vacant. Feeling relieved I stepped inside and closed the door. The room was decked out in a green theme. A hunter green sofa sat to the

186

right against the wall along with two matching chairs and a coffee table. There was a green velvet king-sized bed sitting in the middle of the room with green satin sheets on it. On the nightstand next to the bed were several pleasurables including a dildo, handcuffs, a whip, blindfold, lubricant, and condoms. On the other nightstand were bottles of chocolate, whip cream, and honey. There was a table off to the side with clean linen and towels, wipes, and toy cleaner.

The door to the room opened and a couple of servers walked in carrying a tray of sandwiches and drinks. Seeing the same fruity drinks King handed me, I grabbed the two that were on the tray. "Miss, these are all for you," the one carrying the drink tray said.

"For me? Why all of this for me?"

"Those were the orders we just received," the other server shrugged. They sat the trays on the coffee table then exited the room.

I took a seat on the sofa. I sat one of the drinks I was carrying back onto the tray and grabbed a sandwich. I sat back on the sofa and watched the porno as I ate and drank. I'm not sure how long I had been sitting there but I began to feel tingly all over, especially my sugar box. I was feeling the same way I had at Francois's boutique. The thought of what went down that day had my sugar walls clinching.

My hand had a mind of its own as it brushed across my neck and down my cleavage. I uncrossed my legs and spread them open, placing my feet onto the table. My pussy tingled as I watched a new porn flick that started with a big booty sister giving head to one guy as she got fucked in the ass by another. My fingers found my precious pearl and caressed it sensually. I slid two of my fingers inside my love cave causing my nectar to drizzle out. I played in my pussy and brought myself to an orgasm.

Remembering the dildo on the nightstand, I stood and unzipped my dress. I stepped out of it and laid across the back of the chair as I passed it going over to the bed. I grabbed it and sprayed it down with the cleaner even though it was brand new. You never can be too careful. I wiped it off with one of the towels then grabbed a condom.

I tore the foil and pulled the condom off. I pulled the condom out and rolled it down onto the dildo. I laid across the bed, positioning myself so that I could still watch the flick. I sucked the dildo into my mouth and mimicked what the chick was doing. When she deep-throated the dick, I deep-throated the dildo. I bobbed up and down on the dildo the same time she bobbed up and down on dude's dick. The whole time, I masturbated myself to another orgasm.

Ole girl finally stood and laid on the bed. Dude climbed between her legs then placed them on his shoulders. As he slid his dick inside her, I slid the dildo inside of me. I turned the vibration on to a medium speed. I lifted my legs in the air in a V and thrust the dildo in and out of my pussy at the same speed dude thrust in and out of her.

"Let me help you with that."

My eyes shot opened and I looked over to see King standing just inside the door. Hell, I was so into getting myself off I didn't realize I had closed my eyes, nor did I hear the door open. I licked my lips at the sight of him standing there in..... his pajamas? He had on his pajama pants and matching robe and was still wearing his mask. When did this become a pajama party? Why did it matter to me I had no idea. Let's be real; I'm lying in a bed at a stranger's house fucking myself with a damn dildo! But he was looking so damn fine.

I pulled the dildo out and brought my legs down. I sat up and watched King as he closed the door and locked it. My breathing picked up as I watched King slowly walk towards me. I felt like prey in the enchanted forest about to be devoured by the lion. My juices trickled down my inner thigh, I was so turned on. King stopped at the foot of the bed and let his robe fall off his shoulders onto the floor. He then pulled his pajama pants down and the biggest dick I'd ever seen up close and personal sprang out before me. My pearl throbbed to the point it was hurting. My juices flowed from within me soiling the sheets beneath me.

A moan from the guy getting head on the TV drew my attention. The woman was going to work as she spat on the tip of his dick then sucked him into her mouth. King turned to see what I was looking at. His dick jumped as he watched the woman performing. I crawled over to him and sucked the tip into my mouth. He looked down at me and I could see the surprise in his eyes behind his mask. I winked then put my attention back to the flick. Everything she did, I did to King. When she spit on the dick, so did I. When she tea bagged dude's balls, I did the same to King. "Oh shit!" Both King and dude on the flick called out at the same time.

She used one hand to massage his balls as she used her other hand and jerked him off as she sucked on the tip. And I did the same to King. His ball sack tightened and a few moments after, he released his load and it skeeted down my throat. I drank it all down, slurping, sucking, until I had every drop. I kissed the tip before pulling away from him. I licked my lips to get any remnants that remained.

I smiled and leaned back onto my elbows. King stood there looking down on a word. I spread my legs apart and gave him a full view of my glistening goldmine. My pussy was so wet, my juices were on the inside of my thighs. King knelt down as if he was about to pray, but that was nowhere near what was about to happen. He glanced up at the flick and then back at me. "My turn," he said and buried his face in my safari of love.

He tongued kissed my second set of lips, sucking my clit between his teeth and snaking his long tongue inside my pussy. He zig-zagged his tongue up and down, side to side from my pussy to my ass. I wind my hips along with his tongue actions. I put my hand on the back of his head and pushed him deeper into my wetness as I began to cum all over his tongue. My legs started to shake as he pushed my legs further apart and dipped his tongue in and out of my soaking pussy. "Mmm, yes, like that," I said.

King moaned in my pussy as if this was the best meal he'd ever eaten, and it drove me wild. My orgasms came back to back as he continued to lap up my juices the gushed out into his mouth and down his chin. The sight of that had me coming again. King licked my pussy trying to get every drop of my honey. He licked along my inner thighs, lapping up all remnants of me. "Ooh, fuck!"

"You taste so fucking good." King licked his lips as he stood. He went over to the nightstand and grabbed a condom. I crawled to the head of the bed and watched him tare the foil and sheath his rod with the condom. "Are you ready for the royal treatment, Miss Garrison?"

Instead of responding to him verbally, I laid down on the bed and spread my legs apart. I curled my finger for him to come to me. He did as instructed and climbed between my legs. He pushed my legs further apart with my knees bent back onto the bed and slid inside my wet tunnel. He leaned down and kissed me just as I opened my mouth and gasped. I tasted my nectar on his tongue as he began to thrust inside of me.

He slow grind in and out of me, more like he was making love to me than us fucking, if that makes sense to you. I raked my nails gently up and down his back. I pulled away from the kiss and buried my face in his chest, licking and nibbling on his nipple. "Mmm," King moaned.

He picked up the pace of his thrust and I rotated my hips to match his. I threw my head back onto the pillow when he pushed my knees more into the bed going deeper. "Aah, aah, mmm," I cried out. He was going hella deep. I didn't know if it was pain or pleasure, I was feeling, but either way I didn't want him to stop. He hit a g-spot I didn't know existed and before I knew I gushed all around us!

"Gawdamn!" King shouted. "Shit!"

My voice got caught in my throat from the explosive orgasm. In my mind I was singing several octaves but in reality, no words came out. King kept pounding that spot and I kept gushing. It was like I was a pipe that burst under the kitchen sink and the water splashed out in a rush and then just kept coming. I felt like I was now in a waterbed from the way I was coming.

"Shit, Darcel! Can I cum in this pussy?" King asked as he quickened his pace. I pulled him further into me by his ass and tightened my walls around his dick. I pulsated quickly around him enjoying the feel of my wet tight pussy being massaged internally by his massive dick. "Fuuucck!" King called out as he came inside the condom. I could feel it filling up to the max with his semen.

King pulled out of me then bent down and latched onto my clit with his mouth. I arched my back as he sucked on my precious jewel, sopping up my flavor. I gyrated my pelvis into his mouth as he ate me to another orgasm. I felt like he had licked my soul out of me, and it was standing off to the side watching our sexual fiasco. My eyes rolled to the back of my head as the euphoria took over me. That orgasm damn near took me down for the count. My heart beat so fast, my ears were popping, and I was gasping for air. Blinking fast, I saw stars burst. The bliss of his sex was magnificent.

He finally withdrew his tongue and face from between my sticky thighs. I just lay there, trying to get my breathing under control and calm my legs from shaking. My body was in shock at the activities it had been a part of for the past couple of hours. I was sore, tired, relaxed, but still wanting more all at the same time. How could this be possible?

Perspiration slid down my face and into my eyes making my vision blurry as I watched King moving around. He ripped the condom off and tossed it in the trash can. He then went over to the nightstand and grabbed the purple furry covered handcuffs. I was too tired to even protest when he clasped them around my wrists then pulled my arms over my head. I tugged my arms but to no avail. King had not only handcuffed me, but he also tied me to the bed.

"Wait, King, turn me loose," I begged.

"Oh, baby, we're just getting started," King replied devilishly.

I was scared yet curious at what was to come. He took the bottle of honey and poured it on my breasts, making a trail down to my slick kitty. He poured some on his fingers then painted my lips with them. I sucked the remains off his fingers, and he groaned.

Sounds from the hallway caught our attention when someone turned the knob but couldn't get in because King locked it. They banged on the door a couple of times before he when and opened it. The sound of the music and chatter overshadowed the porno playing on the TV. A couple shoved King to the side as they bombarded their way inside the bedroom.

A shapely woman walked in wearing a long emerald green evening gown with a matching bling mask. Her skin was a dark chocolate and looked flawless. The man with her wore a matching green suit without a shirt and a green hornet's mask. He was tall but not too tall, nice six pack, and brown skinned. The couple was either drunk, high or both. Which was it, I couldn't tell. However, I was pissed I was restrained because I wanted to get the hell out of here.

"Ooh, what do y'all got going on here?" the woman asked slurring her words. Her eyes glistened looking over at me. She came and stood at the end of the bed. Licking her lips, she began to undress. I tugged on the handcuffs trying to get free of them but to no avail. "King, come uncuff me now." Panic filled my voice, but no one seemed to care. The woman climbed onto the bed and forced my legs apart then placed her face between my legs. I tried to resist her but whatever she was doing was feeling so damn good. The way she twirled her tongue around my pearl was pure bliss. Then the way she sucked on my labia and nibbled just on the outside of my pussy had me creaming all over her tongue and face. "Oh god! Umm!"

My eyes fluttered as this drunk woman I never met in my life ate my pussy better than any man I've ever been with, even better than Misty. She was the second woman I've been with and I must say a woman eating pussy is way better than a man. Maybe it's because she knows the most sensitive spot because she's a woman. She knew when and where to apply just the right amount of pressure and when to be gentle. Or maybe it was because she tasted the honey King had just poured down there. Hell, I don't know, but what I knew at that moment was I wouldn't mind having her eat my box out every day for the rest of my life.

King and the man joined us in the festivities. King latched onto one of my nipples as the man stood behind her. "Mmm, daddy," the woman cooed when her man entered her from behind. When she moaned, my pussy tingled from the vibration and with King sucking my nipples I came again. I didn't think I could ever come as much as I came tonight. I've lost count on the number of orgasms I've had.

The woman lifted her head from between my legs when her man began to thrust faster and harder. He was giving her the business too. He smacked her ass and she cried out the sweetest sound. The smirk on his face as he laid the pipe on his woman was the funniest thing ever, but my attention was pulled away when King freed my hands from the cuffs.

I grabbed him and pulled him down onto the bed and straddled him. I slid down his dick and began to ride him. The lady pulled away from her man and laid down on the bed beside King and me. She began sucking her man off. Feeling extra freaky, I positioned myself where I was riding King cowgirl style and spread her legs apart. I leaned down and sniffed her coochie before placing my tongue on her.

I slowly licked her tasting her salty juices. She must have liked what I was doing since she spread her legs further apart. Thinking about how both she and Misty ate me out, I began to mimic them, twirling my tongue and darting it in and out of her pussy hole. Her moans gave me a bit more confidence and I slurped and licked in tune with bouncing up and down King's dick. The room filled with moans, smacks, and bodies pounding.

"Aah, Marie! Baby suck this dick," the man called out.

Marie placed a hand on the back of my head when I sucked hard on her clit. She grinds her pussy into my mouth letting me know I was getting the job done. "Damn, daddy I'm about to cum. Cum with me," Marie said. I felt her ass tightening up and her legs began to shake. Knowing I was the reason she was cumming had my orgasm making its way to the forefront.

King plummeted up in me harder as I came down on him. Ooohs and aahs came out of all of our mouths as we all came simultaneously. Marie skeeted down my throat and all over my face as she came, and I could feel my gushy streaming down King's dick and spilling out onto the bed around us. I looked up from between Marie's legs and her man was shooting his load all over her face and breasts. King pumped a couple of times and he came inside me. I tried to pull off when I realized we fucked without a condom, but he held onto me so tight I couldn't pull away until he was flaccid.

We all pulled away from each other spent and well satisfied. I though, was silently praying to God I wasn't pregnant by this man I knew nothing about. I also prayed I didn't catch some kind of STD from this couple.

I was the first to climb out of bed. I grabbed one of the towels and some wipes off the table and began to clean up. King followed suit but the couple were going at it again. Apparently, he liked to taste his own semen because he was licking Marie's chest and every other place his nut landed on her. I don't know why that disgusted me, but it did.

"Stay with me tonight," King whispered to me. He grabbed some wipes and began to clean himself up as well.

"No, I can't."

"Why?"

"I think tonight was fun enough. I'm tired and would rather go home," I moved around him and picked my dress up off the floor. I stepped into it and zipped it up as far as I could. King stood behind me and zipped me up the rest of the way before he stepped into his pajama pants.

Marie and her man were so into their lovemaking that her mask came off. I gasped when I realized she was Marie Sanchez, the news anchor. Wow! So that meant the man was her husband, high priced defense attorney, Carlos Sanchez. King was right about the type of people who'd be here. To say I was astounded by this revelation was an understatement.

King looked over at them to see what had my attention. He cursed under his lips seeing her mask off. He turned to me and gave me the craziest look as if to warn me to keep my mouth closed about who I saw.

"No worries, like you said, we all have lots to lose if someone knew our identities," I reminded him.

Slipping on my shoes I grabbed my purse and headed for the door. Then something caught my attention. I turned around and to my surprise, King was standing behind me. "This room is green. They are wearing green. Was there a meaning behind this or was that just a coincidence?"

"Both actually. Some of the guests who've been to past events have preferences for certain rooms. They have to bid on the room and whoever wins the bid gets the room. The rooms are then color coordinated and they wear that particular color."

"So, I just so happened to come to this room or was it unlocked specifically for me? I tried to go into several rooms, but the doors were all locked."

"Yes. Since this was your first time, I wanted you to be comfortable and get the best experience. I knew you'd have to be restrained in order to be taken out of your shell. That's why I handcuffed you before they came. I knew if you weren't tied up you wouldn't have gone through with everything."

King was right. Extreme circumstances would have had to occur for me to do what I did tonight just like at that boutique shop. Francoise spiked my drink and had me so horny that I had a threesome and here King handcuffed me since I wasn't drunk enough to just allow a woman or another strange man to just screw me. But how did these men know to do those things to me? Why would they not think I wouldn't have just gone through with these sexual activities just being sober?

"Stay with me, Darcel and I'll explain everything to you," King said. He opened the door and grabbed my hand, but I pulled away.

"There's no need to explain, Kennard. I know who you are and have known for quite some time now. There's no need to rehash the past. It's all water under a bridge now. But I do want to thank you for the most exhilarating experience. Take care," I kissed King on his cheek and walked away leaving him standing there flabbergasted.

Kennard King Stanley was my first love, my first lover, and my first heartbreak. Shit happened in life and we parted ways. Tonight, was closure for me though. As great as the sex was with him, I now know we could never be and I'm quite alright with that.

Chapter 14: All A Dream

Ben and Sabrina lay in his king-sized bed talking and laughing as Usher played in the background. It's been a couple of months since they last saw each other and they carried on conversation after conversation until Sabrina let out a yawn and stretched her 5'5" frame causing her d-sized breast to poke out through the tank top she had on. Ben immediately grabbed a handful and began caressing the right breast as he sucked the left nipple and tugged on it through the tank top.

"Umm," Sabrina moaned and placed a hand on the back of his head. "Baby let me take this top off," she said wiggling underneath Ben's chiseled body. They both sat up and began stripping out of what little clothing they had on. Once naked, Ben grabbed a condom. A big smile spread across Sabrina's face as she has been waiting to take a ride ever since their last encounter.

She seductively crawled to the edge of the bed where Ben stood and began stroking him. He climbed into the bed while Sabrina continued to stroke his massive dick. "Lay back and let me talk into the mic," she said pushing him onto his back.

She was kind of nervous about giving him head for the first time but cheered herself on in her mind. On her knees she leaned down and licked the tip of his dick before taking it into her mouth. Flicking her tongue around the tip, she massaged his balls at the same time. She ran her tongue up and down the shaft before sucking on his balls. As she sucked and tugged on his balls, she stroked his shaft causing a moan to slip out of Ben. Sabrina then took as much of him as she could into her mouth and began bobbing her head up and down until she tasted his precum.

"Ooh," came out of Ben's mouth as Sabrina's head game put some work on his dick. "Sss," he moaned some more.

Knowing her head game had Ben moaning and squirming turned Sabrina on, and she let out a moan her damn self. Shit she damn near came she was so turned on by how she was making him feel. She bobbed her head, licked, and slurped for a few more minutes. She lifted her head smiling. "Put the condom on." Sabrina was so ready that her juices flowed down her inner thigh. "Just watching you put it on got me on fire right now," she crooned.

She climbed on top thinking she was about to take a ride, but Ben had something else in mind. He rolled them over so that he was on top and began sucking on those breasts he seemed to like so much. He kissed his way down her belly and then nibbled on her inner right thigh. He stuck one, then two, fingers inside her wet box and began doing the come here gesture.

"Aahh," Sabrina panted.

"Damn, you're so wet, baby," he said just before stroking his tongue along her folds. Ben licked her pearl while his fingers stroked inside her. Sabrina rotated her hips to match his thrusts.

"You about to make me cum," she purred. "Put it in now," she demanded.

Granting her wish, Ben climbed over her, positioned the head at her opening, and then slammed inside her. "Oh," they both moaned in unison.

"Shit! Do it again," Sabrina squealed. Ben pulled all the way and again slammed inside her. "Yes!" she yelled.

He began stroking his dick inside her slowly, rotating, and hitting Sabrina's spot every time. Ben buried his face in the crook of her neck and sucked on her flesh. "You feel so good," he whispered in her ear. He took her left leg and hooked it over his right arm as he stroked longer and deeper hitting the bottom of Sabrina's pussy.

"Ooh! Ahhh! Ahhh! I'm about to come!" Sabrina yelled as her legs began to shake and her pussy muscles clamped onto Ben's dick like a vice grip.

"Shit, baby," Ben yelled and picked up the pace. "Fuck!" He let out as his nut came up. He pumped a couple more times and nutted inside the condom. "Shit, Sabrina," he said releasing the last load before collapsing on top of her.

They lay that way for a couple of seconds trying to catch their breath. Ben leaned up and kissed Sabrina on her lips before crawling out the bed and heading into the bathroom. Sabrina laid with her legs still open still trying to come down from her high. "Come take a shower a with me," Ben called from the bathroom.

Sabrina reluctantly climbed out of bed and made her way into the bathroom. Ben had already turned the water on and was stepping inside the tub when she walked in. Sabrina sat on the toilet and handled her business before joining him. They washed each other while at the same time turning each other on again.

"Let's get back in bed. I haven't smacked that ass yet," Ben said ushering Sabrina out of the tub.

She giggled as she ran into the bedroom and hopped onto the bed. She positioned herself on all fours with her back arched and ass tooted in the air. She looked back at Ben wiggling her ass. "Is this how you want it, daddy?" she asked.

Ben nodded his head yes as he grabbed a condom and slipped it on. Standing behind a wet and waiting ass, he slapped the right cheek and Sabrina's pussy muscles began to contract. "Umm," she moaned. Whack! Another slap onto the left ass cheek and she came right then and there. Ben watched as her sweet serum trickled down onto the bed from her love canal. His dick rocked up even more. Ben squeezed both ass cheeks and then smacked the right cheek again. "That's some sexy shit I tell ya!"

"I need it in me! Give it to me, baby," Sabrina begged. She was panting, so you would have thought she ran a damn marathon she was so turned on. Ben placed the tip just inside and taunted her. "Stop playing and give it to me," Sabrina whined.

"You about to say my name," Ben stated and rammed inside her causing a gurgling moan to come out. He smacked her ass as he stroked that pussy fast, long, and deep. Sabrina got in sync with him and began backing that big ass up on him.

"Oh yes," she screamed.

"Say my name," Ben demanded and smacked her ass.

"Ooh Ben! Ben! Ben!" Sabrina belted out. She twerked her ass fast and then slow and twirled it around getting a few moans among some other sounds out of Ben.

"Yea, take this dick!" Whack! Whack! More smacks to Sabrina's ass and her orgasm rushed on her so fast, her words were caught in her throat. Her pussy muscles swallowed up Ben's dick and choked it until he let loose his nut into the condom.

Then I woke up with my fingers in my pussy and the spot underneath me soaked only to realize this was all a dream. Damn!

Chapter 15: Chaos

It has been weeks since I last saw you. I don't understand why we can't get this shit right. For just a few moments, I'm happy to see you, but just as quickly I'm ready for you to leave. The routine never changes; we fuss then fuck, fuck and fuss some more. It's pure chaos but I can't seem to let you go. Is it because of how well you know my body? How no man can make me react the way you do? I wish like hell I can figure this out so I can be rid of you. My problem though is that I'm a married woman and you are my husband's friend.

But, how can I? Every time I make my mind up to leave, you come in and make the sweetest love to me, whisper sweet nothings in my ear, make me have orgasm after orgasm. As I lay here now, I think back to the day I met you. Oh, how timid and naïve I was. I was so young, fifteen to be exact. The new kid on the block and not knowing a soul, I sat on the porch watching you and your friends in your yard across the street doing the latest dance moves to the hottest songs.

You did a move then hit a back flip and landed on your feet. I was so impressed! The girls who were there acted like some groupies as they cheered you on. The guys all gave you dap and props for hitting such a smooth move. It wasn't until my dad pulled into the driveway that any of you looked over in my direction. We locked eyes and I felt a surge of electricity flow through me. For just a few moments life itself stopped and it was just you and I together in that moment. I felt it, and I could tell you did too. The connection that will forever bind us together was made on that day eighteen years ago.

You made your way across the street and introduced yourself to my dad before coming onto the porch and introducing yourself to me. Marcus Deshawn Carter, you told me with your hand held out. You invited me to come hang out with you and your friends. With a head nod from Dad, I accepted and that changed my life.

We became the best of friends that day. Not too long after we became a couple. I could tell your crew wasn't too happy about you placing all your attention on me. Your groupies didn't like that not one bit, but I gave zero fucks about them. Your homeboys were pissed because you made it clear to them that I was off limits. I was in La La Land, head over hills in love with you, Marcus. I would fight and kick any bitch's ass that tried to come for me over you. I turned down every guy that stepped to me because he wasn't you.

And when I finally gave myself to you sexually, I never knew pain could feel so damn good. It was our senior prom. I wore an elegant long sleeves lilac mermaid dress that accentuated my figure to perfection. You wore a tuxedo that matched my dress with a black shirt and tie. You looked debonair! My kitty melted inside my panties in anticipation for what the night was to bring.

We were voted prom king and queen, you because of your popularity, and me by default for being your girlfriend. We danced and partied the night away until it was time to head to our room you got us for the night. Being it was our senior prom; my parents were actually lenient and allowed me to stay out all night. Besides, I was already named Valedictorian of the senior class and I had scholarships upon scholarships to damn near any college I wanted to attend.

In our room you ran us a hot bath and filled the tub with lavender scented bath oil. Somehow you used your charm and had a bottle of champagne on chill with some hors d'oeuvres. I could tell you put so much thought into making the night special for me, being that I was a virgin and you had been with the bitch, Rhonda Snell, before you and I met.

I remember gulping down the whole glass of champagne before I allowed you to undress me. I was so nervous to let you see me naked for the first time. Hell, I was nervous to see you naked for the first time. None of our friends ever believed we had never gone past kissing. Little did they know, you were patient and understanding towards me back then. Somehow that all went away over the years and I wonder why.

We finally stood completely naked in front of each other for the first time and I was frightened at the size of your penis. It was humongous to me being that I had never seen a dick up close and personal before that night. You assured me you'd fit inside me, but I had my doubts. Nevertheless, I was ready to give myself to you completely.

First you bathe me from head to toe. Then you sat on the edge of the tub as I stood in front of you. You placed one of my legs over your shoulder and buried your face between my legs. Oh, what a feeling it was. Your tongue snaked in my precious place, licking my essence of pleasure. The feeling was amazing. You latched on to my pearl and sucked her into submission, marking your territory. I panicked when I felt my first orgasm coming to the front. It felt like I needed to pee, and I tried to pull away, but you held me tightly in place and I let loose all over your mouth and face. I came so hard and long; I damn near collapsed on you.

When you came up for air with a huge smile plastered on your face, I felt relief. You explained to me I had nothing to feel ashamed of for gushing all over your face, that it was normal when I have orgasms. You said that would help make it easier when you entered me. I didn't believe you, but I went along with it anyways. We washed up again and got out of the tub.

We climbed into bed and you kissed my body from head to toe. You once again went down and kissed the softest place on earth, causing a volcanic eruption yet again. I didn't think I would be able to take much more after that orgasm. It took so much out of me. I just wanted to go to sleep, but you climbed on top of me and penetrated me. As wet as I was, I was still too tight, and it felt as if you were ripping me a new asshole as you entered me inch by inch.

I dug my nails into your back as I hung on for dear life as you broke through my hymen. Tears ran down my face from the pain. I begged you to wait until the pain subsided before continuing on. You granted my request and after a few minutes my pussy muscles were contracting around you, giving you the green light to proceed. I was in heaven as you made love to me. Your thrust was not too hard, not too deep, but just right. And you seem to find my spot with no problem, as if you knew where to aim all along. My, my, my; Marcus you made me call your name and profess that this pussy would always, and forever be yours. You damned right it was yours from that day forward.

After you made me cum two more times, you finally bust your nut inside me. Not once did we even think of wearing protection. I was blinded by love, and you just didn't want to say you wanted to really feel me and wouldn't be able to with the condom. Not once did I think I'd get pregnant my first-time having sex. Oh, how naïve was I.

Our second round of love making, though, you were not as gentle as before. No, you gave it to me hardcore, thrusting deeper, longer, harder, but dammit if it didn't feel good. I found myself trying to match you stroke for stroke and when you flipped me over and entered me from behind, I thought I had died and gone to heaven. Doggystyle has always been my favorite position with you. I got every inch and was filled to the max by you.

After our prom night, our lives changed. Eight weeks later we would find out I was pregnant. Lucky for the both of us, we would have graduated from high school and would be heading to college on full scholarships. The issue we had though was that you were going to Southern University in Louisiana and I would remain in Atlanta at Spellman. My parents refused to allow me to follow you to Southern. Even though we were about to have a child together, they wanted me to follow through with my plan of graduating from Spellman with my bachelor's in health science and continuing on to Georgia State for my master's in health administration.

You had your football scholarship and from the talks you would eventually go pro and be drafted into the NFL. We, well I, had to make the hardest decision of my life and have an abortion. It was the best for everyone, you and our parents convinced me. Lord knows I didn't want to get rid of my baby, but I was out voted by everyone. I was more heartbroken that you didn't want our love child.

We ended up going our separate ways to college. You promised we'd still make our relationship work, but I knew that was a lie. I lost you the day I told you I was pregnant. Yet, I remained faithful to you when we went off to college until a news story broke out that you'd gotten that bitch, Rhonda Snell pregnant and was leaving Southern to go to the NFL.

The day the news broke, so did I. I said fuck you, fuck my parents, fuck school, fuck everything! I got buck wild and got turned out. I began sleeping with guys and girls, no matter their color. I let half of the football team do me in every hole they could fit their dicks into. Shit I even fucked a couple of the fraternity entire line of pledges. I was lucky the only disease I caught back then was chlamydia.

At one point I was placed on academic probation and was damn near kicked out of school. You never got to see the damage you caused me when you sided with me getting an abortion and then leaving me only to get another woman pregnant. I had a nervous breakdown from the pain you caused me. I had no one because I no longer spoke to my family. I was all alone. My life became so chaotic that it took a perfect stranger speaking the truth about me and the path my life was about to head down if I didn't get my shit together.

I eventually pulled myself up by the bootstraps and finished college cum laude, going on to get my masters and doctorate. You went on to marry Rhonda, have three children, and played in the NFL for six years before an injury took you out of the game. As my life was going well, yours was spiraling out of control. You and Rhonda divorce. I finally met Taurus, fell in love, and we got married. You ended up on TMZ and other gossip sites for drugs and alcohol. Taurus and I had a set of twins. My life was going fine until you came back to Atlanta and sought me out.

Why did I allow you back into my life? If Taurus wasn't being such a damn groupie when he opened the door and saw you standing there, none of the events that took place afterwards would have happened. He had no idea the effect you had on me and that you are walking across the threshold of our front door was the biggest mistake he let happen.

You came in with the intentions of breaking up my happy home. I could see it in your eyes. My mind said no, but my heart and body were in agreeance with you. You befriended my husband, got in good with him and let him get too comfortable allowing you to be around us. I tried to warn him of your deceit, but he wouldn't listen. I told Taurus if he didn't get you away from me, you and I would end up hurting him in the end because I knew you would make your move the first chance you had.

Taurus wouldn't believe me. His ego and his bromance for you overshadowed all I warned him of. And just as I predicted, you came over after the two of you had a night out on the town. Taurus was so drunk, high, or both, that you had to carry him inside the house and put him in bed.

You showed no remorse or care in the world as you walked up on me and took me in your arms, kissing me passionately like the long-lost lovers we were. I tried to resist but the more I fought the more my body responded to you. Before I knew it, you had me naked on the sofa, eating my hot box as if it were your last supper. You sucked my pleasure button into your mouth, and I came on contact. I can't deny how good your oral game was feeling. I couldn't suppress my moans as you pleasured me with your mouth, spelling your name out on my pussy, reclaiming what was once yours.

You finally came up and climbed on top of me, sliding in with the quickness. I protested since you weren't wearing a condom, but you had already dipped in and were hitting my spot like only you know how. We forgot all about Taurus as you placed my legs behind my head and long stroked me deep. I called out your name in pleasurable pain. You leaned down and sucked my bottom lip into your mouth and we shared a kiss that words couldn't explain. Our tongues intertwined with one another, getting reacquainted.

I felt my second orgasm arise. I grabbed one of the throw pillows and bit down on it to silence my moans and screams as I came hard. My pussy throbbed and contracted around your massive dick, but you wouldn't come. You wanted me to come again and so you continued to hit my spot, sending those same electric currents I felt the first time our eyes met. I once again came, but my sounds were no longer suppressed by the pillow. I screamed your name over and over until you finally bust your nut inside me.

You'd think Taurus would have woken up from my screams, but he didn't. As we lay on the sofa the only sounds that could be heard were us catching our breath. I don't know what came over me though, but I had you get up and then I led you to the guest bedroom. I laid you on the bed and climbed between your legs. I never had ever given you head and wanted to display my skills to you. I take you in my mouth and deep throat every ten inches of you. You moan in pleasure and I feel my second set of lips drool from your response.

I slurp along your shaft, running my tongue along the long vein from base to tip. I suck hard then soft on the tip, allowing my saliva to spill out down upon you. I taste your precum and how delectable you taste. It's not too salty like Taurus'. Yours has a little sweetness to it. Perhaps it's from whatever you ate or drank today. I like it and I want more, so I bob up and down, running my hand up and down until you come in my mouth. You moan my name as you emptied your load down my throat. I drank every drop of you.

I take you out of my mouth and climb on top of you and place my pussy on your face. You eagerly open your mouth to receive me. I grind my pussy on your mouth as you tongue kiss her. You lick my inner walls lapping up my juices as they rain down. I grab my breasts and squeeze them as I ride your face. I yelp when you place your tongue in my asshole and dart it in and out. On instinct, I began to rub my clit as you ate my ass. My legs began to shake as I came. My honey drizzled out so fast and hard I thought you would drown from my gushy.

I crawled down and grabbed your dick, positioning him at my opening, no longer caring about a condom. I slid down upon you and began to ride you. Shit I missed this dick. After all these years, you were still the best I ever had, yes even better than Taurus. I ride you and we stare in each other's eyes the entire time. You tell me you love me and how much you missed me. You tell me you regret telling me to get an abortion. You apologize over and over as I ride you to another orgasm.

Tears of pain and pleasure stream down my face. I'm beyond ecstatic hearing you say these things that I longed to hear. I can't even respond because I am crying so hard, yet I continue to ride you, picking up the pace. You pump up inside of me as I come down on you. The wave of passion we are on is magical.

The room is filled with our essence and I feel no remorse as I fuck you. All the years we missed out on were brought back to us as we gave in to our desires. You flip me on my back without us even detaching and thrust deep inside of me. I gasp as I feel you in my guts. You quickly pull out and toss me on my stomach. I arched my back and tooted my ass in the air, wanting, waiting for you to enter me from behind.

You surprise me though when you run the tip up and down my asshole. I tense up when you try to enter. You tell me to relax. I fear you're going to bust me open because you're so big. But I follow your instructions and try my best to relax. You help by placing two fingers inside my pussy and finger me as you enter my ass. You ease your way in inch by inch. This takes me back to our first time together when I lost my virginity to you. Just as you were back then, you are gentle as you enter me. Once you are all the way in you don't move. You continue to finger fuck my pussy and it's a feeling I can't even explain.

Being filled in both holes at the same time feels so amazing. It hasn't been since my college days when I was in my whoring phase that I had both pussy and ass filled. I began to rock back and forth on you. You began to match my thrust. Before long we are going at it hard. You slap my ass cheeks and I cry out in pleasure. I demand you go harder and faster. I grab a hold of the edge of the mattress and throw my ass on you. My back is arched more, and I can feel you more in my ass.

You pull my head back by my hair and pound deep inside me. The smacking sounds of our bodies penetrate the walls of the room along with our moans. Ooh you feel so amazing! I can feel my orgasm coming up from my ass shooting up to the crown of my head and rushing back down to my toes and out my pussy as I slushed all around us in the bed. I gushed so hard your fingers were shoved out of my pussy.

I bounce faster on your dick as I can feel your nut building up. The tip of your dick throbbed inside my ass like a beating drum as you came long and hard inside of me. I can feel your load shooting through the walls of my anus and spill out along with my come onto the bed. We both fall forward with you on top of and still inside of me. You continue to pump inside of me until you are completely empty.

For a while, we lay in each other's arms, no words spoken, just in our own thoughts. I am wondering what the hell was I thinking allowing all of this to go down. I tried to tell my husband it wasn't a good idea for me to be in close proximity with you because I knew this would happen. I knew I would not be able to resist you. You knew this as well, and that's why you bombarded my life the way you had.

So now where do we go from here? I cannot continue on in my marriage knowing I just fuck the love of my life in the room down the hall from the one I share with my husband. I cannot just get out of this bed I'm lying in now and go lay next to Taurus. We didn't think nor care about the consequences we now must face behind our actions.

Will you leave me again? Will you stay? Will you love me the way I deserve, or did I just ruin my life once again because of you? Unfortunately, I received my answer when I wake up the next day and find you gone and my husband standing next to the bed you and I made love in just a few hours ago.

I see the hurt in his eyes. They are red from crying. I broke my husband's heart. I am once again a dirty whore. I don't even bother trying to explain. There's no need. The proof is in our scent that lingers in the room and me sprawled out in the bed's still damp sheets from our fluids. The only thing I can do now is to get up, get dressed, and pack a bag. I now have to find a new home because of the chaos I made by fucking you.

Chapter 16: The Tasty Peach

"Welcome all you playas, pimps, hustlers, and hoes! Thanks for coming out to the world renowned and infamous Tasty Peach Gentleman's Club where you will find big booty hoes, from Black to White, to the Asian persuasions. From ten until midnight we got the five-dollar tabletop, but if you want that one on one special that'll cost ya. So, sit back, relax, get ya dollas ready and don't get fucked up touchin. Security is on deck. Oh, and make sure you thirsty bastards tip my waitresses and bartenders. First coming to the stage is the voluptuous, sexy, double dipped chocolate drop that have all you muthafuckas sitting on swole before she even takes her thong off. Y'all give it up for Silky," DJ Domino spat through the mic.

Applause and cat calls rang out as I stood at the end of the stage in a sexy pose. Def Leppard's Pour Some Sugar on Me blasted through the speakers. It was my signature song with a twist. DJ Domino remixed the rock song with a hip hop beat just for me and the crowd always went wild. I sashayed to the center of the stage and grabbed the pole with the cloth in my hand. I twerked my ass as I wiped down the pole, then I tossed the cloth toward the back of the stage. Just as the lyrics stated I wore a red thong and matching bikini top. A pair of clear six-inch strappy stilettos showed off my freshly pedicured feet and fire engine red polish on my toes. Red laying against my silky, chocolate skin always drove both men and women wild.

I hadn't even begun to dance, and they were already tossing money onto the stage. Those bills weren't dollars either. They were fives, tens, and some twenties. This indicated they didn't want to waist anytime getting their entire show without me being naked. Also, I, Samyrah Silky Jessop, was the showstopper at the Tasty Peach. Men from all over came here just to see me dance. I can't lie some were blessed to even get a taste of my peach. However, there hadn't been one to lock me down. They all have tried and failed. It's not that I don't want a man. I just don't want a man who is intimidated about my success and business savvy.

You see not only am I a dancer at the Tasty Peach, I am actually the owner. Yep, you read that right. I started dancing at sixteen when my mom kicked me out after I told her the sorry man, she called her boyfriend touched me inappropriately. She believed him over me, and I became homeless at that point. DJ Domino, who's been more like a brother to me was the only person to know what I was going through. We lived in the same projects and when he caught me sleeping in the stairwell one night, he took me in and got me the job at the club. Of course, he hooked me up with a fake ID since I was underage, but he changed my life. It wasn't called the Tasty Peach back then. Back then it was called Exquisite and owned by Johnny Ellis.

I danced three nights a week and went to school until I graduated high school. DJ stressed to me getting my high school diploma instead of a GED was best for when I decided to leave the club and get a regular job. He even stressed me going on to college and getting a degree. He always said, "Don't be one of those dumb, broke bitches shaking their ass in the club every night and don't have any real shit to show for it."

During that time, I saved every dime I had after I paid DJ for room and board. I followed his advice and didn't do like most of the strippers did and spend my money on unnecessary shit, buying expensive clothes and shoes, expensive cars and not have a pot to piss in. Nope. The day I graduated from high school, I paid cash for a two-bedroom condo downtown and moved out of DJ's crib. I registered for college and paid cash for the semester. I continued to work nights at the club while going to school during the day. I paid cash for every semester and four years later, I graduated with my bachelor's in business administration. That same year, I negotiated a deal with Johnny and bought him out. I changed the name to the Tasty Peach and brought DJ in as the face of the club. I did give him a piece of the business since it was him who got me the job here in the first place. So, besides DJ, the only other person who knows I own the place is the house mother, Ms. Debra, the manager, Ken, and the security team.

So, here I was swaying my hips to the beat of the music as I moved to one side of the stage. I turned my back to the crowd and began twerking my ass just as the chorus kicked in. I dropped to my knees and popped one ass cheek then the other while undoing my thong. I crawled over to the pole, grabbed it, and hoisted myself up. The thong fell from between my legs and more money was tossed onto the stage. I swung my leg around the pole and turned myself upside down. I undid my bikini top and tossed it out in the crowd. I slid down the pole until my hands were flat on the floor, then flipped over into a split.

I crawled over to the one side of the stage and got up close and personal with some of the patrons. I got in a squat position and twerked my ass, opening and closing my legs allowing them a sneak peak of my satin sensation. I let a couple them place money in my garter belt and they copped a feel of my smooth thigh. I then made my way to the pole and climbed up. I swung around until I was once again upside down but with my heels touching the ceiling. I walked around the pole a couple of times.

"Yo, y'all know Silky is the shit! Toss some more bills of you want to see her hit the infamous split upside down on the ceiling!" DJ Domino belted over the music.

It began to rain dollars as Def Leppard ended and Rhianna's Pour It Up started. When I saw the crowd was doing just that, I hit my signature move swinging around on the pole, grabbing a hold of the metal beam, and breaking into a split upside down. I twerked my ass for several seconds before grabbing the pole and sliding down until I was midway. I then wrapped my arms onto the pole and swung my legs out and underneath me so that I was right side up again. I swung around until my feet were back on the stage.

I twirled around and ran my hands down my body seductively. I placed a hand on one of my breasts and the other on my mound, motioning as if I was about to masturbate in front of them when a tall brown skinned guy with muscles for days approached the end of the stage. Dude was just too damn fine for no reason! Whew! His eyes bore into me and held my gaze as he began tossing out all the bills he had in his hand. He smiled the most gorgeous smile the entire time.

I got down on my knees and laid on my back. I sat up on my elbows and pulled my legs up in the air. I spread them apart, wiggling them causing my ass to jiggle in the process. Money man stood there getting a full view of my pussy. Shit with all the money he was shelling out I had no problem letting him get all in it. When he licked his lips and winked, it took everything in me not to come. I rotated so that I was face down, ass up and simulated throwing my ass back on a dick I was fucking.

"Y'all give it up for Silky," DJ Domino announced letting me know my session was over. A couple of the bouncers came over to assist me with picking up all the money. Thanks to Mr. Money Man, I had three trash bags full of cash by the time we'd picked up all the bills off the stage and the floor.

"Yo, Silky, Muscle Man is asking for a private one on one with you," Selena, a waitress stopped me as I was making my way back to the locker room.

"Aiight. You got some info on him?"

"He's new in town to take over his uncle's business. What business that is? I don't know. But what I do know is he is loaded and has a large entourage with him."

"Okay—" Selena waved her hand around and nodded her head cutting me off.

"Yes, they are all spending mad money. Whatever business he's here to take over, is bringing in mad cash flow Dude has shelled out ten grand just on the liquor alone."

"Thanks, Lena. Put him in my VIP room and make sure he's comfortable until I get there. Whatever he wants, get it for him," I instructed but she waved her hand around again.

"Already done."

"Cool. Thanks!" I hurried to the locker room and to my personal vanity space. Beast, my security guard stood next to me as I placed the three trash bags inside my suitcase and secured it. He then took my suitcase and carried it to the main office where DJ would place it in the safe. If something was to ever happen to my money, I know it would be a set up by DJ since he was the only person besides me that had access to the safe. Not even Ken had access and he was the manager.

Anyway, I went through my outfits and chose a purple string bikini set with a matching wrap. I went and hopped in the shower and washed up before oiling my body with shea butter. I sprayed on some Betsey Johnson perfume. Besides lip gloss and eyeliner, I didn't wear any other makeup since I didn't need it, but I always felt gritty after a while of constant dancing. Besides it just took too much time to apply and reapply throughout the night.

I got dressed, brushed my hair down and tossed it over one shoulder before heading to the VIP room. For some strange reason I had butterflies floating in my belly. I didn't know what that was about, but I was about to find out. Beast was already posted up outside the door when I walked up. That's why he was my A1. I hardly had to dish out orders to him. He was always several steps ahead of me and I appreciated that about him. He gave me a head nod then knocked on the door once. He opened it up and stood to the side so I can enter.

"She is precious cargo, so act like you know and don't get fucked up," Beast said and walked out closing the door behind him before Mr. Money Man could respond.

"Is he your bodyguard or your man?" Mr. Money Man's deep voice vibrated through my sacred placed.

"He's only my bodyguard but everyone here would come at you that way if they hadn't already," I said.

"I'm sure they would be since you're the boss."

"And where did you get that info from?"

"My uncle Johnny. He told me years ago when he sold this place to you. I was pissed off about it at first because I wanted to take over when he was ready to give it up, but he felt your offer was much better." Mr. Money Man took a seat on the sofa. He grabbed the bottle of Hennessey and poured some in a cup.

"Is that why you're here? And what's your name by the way?"

"My name is Bartholomew, but you can call me Big B. And no, I'm not here about your business."

"Okay, Big, then why are you here?"

"Hmp, Johnny warned me about you."

"What is that supposed to mean?"

"He said you were hell on wheels, did shit your way, and didn't care."

"Oh really? Well that's because I had to keep nuccas in line that came at me wrong, and my way always worked. However, if I didn't care then I'd be like half of these bitches around here, broke, and sucking dick for five dollars. So, trust me Mr. Bartholomew, I care."

"Well, Ms. Samyrah, since we are going by our government names, I came here for you. Uncle J always talked about you. He had the upmost respect for you. He liked how you moved while working under him. Oh, and he knew your ass was underage when that nigga Domino brought you here. He told my uncle what was up with you and my uncle said he saw that determination in your eyes to make something out of yourself by any means necessary. That's why he sold the club to you."

I stood there in awe as to what Johnny had to say about me. I honestly didn't think the man liked me but hearing all this I had a newfound respect for the man. I went and took a seat on the sofa next to Bartholomew. I grabbed the bottle of Hennessey and poured myself a shot. I tossed it down then poured another one. I was about to take that shot but he took it out of my hand.

"Nah, shorty, you don't need that. I want you sober for what's about to go down," Bartholomew said.

"What's about to go down?"

"Oh, I'm about to show you why they call me Big B," he smirked.

"I thought it was because of all these muscles."

"Oh, that's just part of the package, baby."

"And how do you figure any of that shit is about to go down with me? I'm pretty sure Johnny told you it's very rare that I do VIP and when I do, you only get dances, nothing more," I was offended and turned on at the cockiness of his ass thinking I was just going to lay down and open my legs up for him. Well, technically I already did, but what I meant was to let him in between them.

"When you were up on that stage, I could tell you wanted me just as much as I want you. You may have fooled them niggas out there, but you can't fool me. I can smell your sex right now and it's calling my name."

"That's the craziest shit I have ever heard," I laughed,

"Tell me that pussy ain't wet right now," Bartholomew moved closer to me. I turned my head and bit down on my lip. I couldn't lie because my pussy was drenching the seat of my thong in that very moment. "Mmm, just what I thought," I turned back to see that cocky grin in his face.

"Whatever. Do you want a dance or not?"

"Yeah, I want a dance, but you can just go ahead and take all that off now. I want you in your birthday suit."

"You do know you have forty-five minutes, right?"

"Nah, Silky, I paid for the time to have this room with you for the rest of the night which by my watch is three hours." Bartholomew looked at his blinged out Rolex watch that back up at me.

"Fine," I stood and went over to the wall where the sound system was and turned the music up to what DJ was playing.

"Nah, put that on Pandora to the slow jams station." I scrunched my face up at his request. "I'm the client, baby. It's what I request," Bartholomew smirked again.

I didn't bother to respond. I did as he asked, and R. Kelly's Twelve Play came on. I didn't bother to turn around until I had taken off what little piece of clothing I had on. I sat them neatly on the table in front of me then turned to face Bartholomew. "Do you want me to dance now or do you want to just fuck?"

"Is this how you treat all your clients when you're in the VIP?"

"Pretty much. Like I said I don't typically fuck. I can really count on one hand and have fingers left over as to the number of guys who's had the pleasure to be privileged enough to sniff my goodies. Not every stripper is a prostitute or a whore, THOT, or cokehead as many people think."

"I never called you that nor do I think any of that about you. However, I want to fuck you. And I don't usually go to strip clubs looking for pussy. It's just that the pussy I want happens to be at one at the time."

"What the hell? So, you really think you got it like that, huh?"

"I know I do. Samyrah, I can have any woman I want with no questions. I know I'm a good-looking brother. I have big dick and money to match. I'm the total package. I don't go looking for pussy. Pussy comes to me."

"Yet here you are looking to get my pussy. I can admit your cockiness turns me on. I assure you if you wasn't as fine as you are and had you not just paid my newly purchased whip off with all that you've spent at my club tonight, I would be sending your ass out of here with hurt feelings and blue balls. But since you filled a bitch's purse so generously, I'm going to go along with your little plans. Now let's get this shit poppin."

I moved over to the bed and climbed in. I laid on my back and spread my legs in a seductive manner. Bartholomew's eyes glossed over as he took in my wet pussy glistening for him. He took another shot of Hennessey then began to undress. I rubbed on my clit as I watched him undress. Damn, this mother lover is foine with a capital F! I felt my nipples hardened at the site of his huge muscular arms and chest. His six-pack looked 3D he was so ripped. And when he stepped out of his pants and boxers, I came.

His dick was huge! It was so goddam pretty. He was clean shaven and no shave bumps in site. His dick was the same brown complexion as the rest of his body with a lighter tone at the tip where he was circumcised. That thing had to have been a good eleven inches and it didn't even appear to be hard. My damn! I don't know if I can take all of that, but I wasn't a punk. I was sure as hell about to give it a try.

Bartholomew stood at the end of the bed stroking himself. He smiled that gorgeous smile at me as he climbed in the bed and between my legs. Shit, his dick was at my pussy before he was fully between my legs. The tip pressed against my nub and had me on edge. My breathing quickened and we hadn't done anything yet. Bartholomew rubbed the tip between my lips, teasing my pearl here and there. I grind against the tip wanting him inside me.

"Can I put him in?" Bartholomew asked. It was crazy for him to ask when he had already placed the tip at my opening and was easing his way inside my tunnel.

"Ooh, umm," I moaned as he slid further inside of me. I placed my hand on his stomach when I felt him in my belly.

"Awe, what? You can't take all of him?"

"Nope. You're already in my stomach," I admitted with no shame.

"We gonna have to work on that then. Sss, mmm, you feel so good, Samyrah."

Bartholomew began slow stroking me deep as I would allow him. He stretched and filled me to the max. He felt so good, but it also hurt so bad at the same time. Tears ran down my face and I wasn't sure if they were from pain, pleasure, or both. Either way, he was thrusting in and out and causing friction on my clit while hitting my g-spot. My entire body began to shake as my orgasm built up.

"Aah, aah, ooh, uuh," I moaned loudly.

"Shit, yeah, baby. Let that shit go," Bartholomew said as he pulled out and buried his face into my pussy. He sucked on my clit and lapped up my juices as I began to come. He stuck his long tongue inside my pussy, and I lost all senses. I have never had a tongue that damn long and big inside of my coochie. But what a wonderful feeling it was. I rained down on his tongue and he sucked it all up, drinking every drop of my honey.

I placed both hands on the back of his head and held him in place as a second orgasm crushed me like an ocean hitting the shore of a beach. I rode his tongue until it felt raw. I didn't even have to tell him to put his enormous dick back inside me. It was like he knew my body's reaction and didn't hesitate to slide back inside of me.

This time around I couldn't feel him in my stomach so much even though he was deep inside. I met him with each thrust when he placed me in the buck and went to town. He sat up and spread my legs apart. He was on his knees pumping in and out fast and hard. I placed my fingers on my clit and played with her as he fucked me into submission. Shit I was about ready to have his babies he was fucking me so good.

When I felt another orgasm coming on, I rubbed on my clit faster and tried to match his thrust. Bartholomew placed my legs on his shoulders then pushed them back to where my knees were damn near parallel to my breast. He pulled my arms in and held them in place with his hands on the bed. I couldn't move at all. All I could do was hold on to his thighs as he pumped in me briskly. He fed me his entire dick and I felt him in my guts!

"Oh, shit, ah, B-bar-tho-lo-meeew! Ahhh, shit!"

"Yes, baby! Say my name!"

Blood must have rushed to my ears because I could barely hear, my heart was pounding so loudly. My vision became blurry and my body began to feel numb as a massive orgasm shot through me. My mouth became dry. I felt like I was saying something but couldn't hear the words coming out of my mouth. From what I could see through my blurred vision, Bartholomew's mouth was moving but I couldn't hear shit he was saying. The next thing I saw was black.

When I regained consciousness, I was laying on Bartholomew's chest. I have no idea how long I was out. My body was sore, and I had a headache. I blinked several times to get my vision clear before I tried to sit up.

"You can't be passing out on a brother while we are getting our freak on," Bartholomew joked.

"Whatever. How long was I out?"

"Only ten minutes."

"It seems longer than that."

"We're gonna have to work on this sex thing. I can't have you clumping out on me every time we are fucking. I need to be able to bust a nut too," I hollered in laughter at him because of that serious look on his face. "That shit ain't funny. I'm serious as fuck! My dick is still hard because I didn't get off."

"Like who says some shit like that? Dude, I could have died from fucking with you. Do you not care about that?"

"Hell yeah, I care. Shit they may try to hem a brother up for some shit I ain't do if that was to happen. But the fact is you didn't die and my dick still hard. I don't want you to suck my dick, I need to bust off in yo' pussy. That's real talk, shorty," Bartholomew said. "Shit roll over on your side and let's try this shit again."

He sat up waiting for me to get in position. I looked at him like he was crazy. He didn't pay my look any attention. He was dead ass serious about getting his nut. I looked down at his dick and that bad boy was hard and ready to do some more damage. I could see all the veins popping out. I looked back up at Bartholomew and he was frowning. I couldn't help but laugh at that look he gave me. Nevertheless, I turned over on my side and raised my leg.

He grabbed a hold of that leg and eased inside me. He stroked long and steady. I matched his strokes and tightened my pussy muscles around him. This time wasn't about me getting off. I wanted to make sure he got his in. I found myself picking up the pace and throwing my pussy on his dick. Now I can get down with him in this position. He was deep inside of me, but it wasn't painful like before.

"Sss, yes, Samyrah. Fuck this dick, baby! Make me cum in your pussy," Bartholomew cheered me on. I grind my pussy and tightened my muscles around him more. The sloshing sound of his dick going in and out of my wet pussy turned me on and I grind harder, faster meeting his every thrust.

"Fuck! Got damn! I'm about to come!" Bartholomew announced. Within seconds he was releasing his semen by the bucket loads. His body shook violently as he nutted. His face twitched up and his eyes rolled to the back of his head. My pussy contracted as he filled me with his sperm.

When his body stopped shaking, he rubbed my clit and I came just as quickly. Even though he had nutted I could still feel him inside of me, he was just that damn big. I rode his semi-hard dick until my orgasm subsided. Then we just laid there catching our breath.

"Samyrah, you got some pussy that's like sunshine!" Bartholomew joked stealing that line from the movie, Harlem Nights.

"You're hilarious," I laughed.

"But for real, shorty, I want to get to know you outside this here club. Real talk, I've been checking you for long time. Like I said earlier, my Uncle Johnny spoke highly of you. I stayed in the background getting a feel for you. I did my research and liked your whole vibe. Trust me if I thought you were like these bitches that work for you, I wouldn't have come up in here at all. But I'm feeling you and want to see what this can lead to," Bartholomew spoked candidly about me.

I didn't rush to say anything because I needed time to process everything. It was one thing hooking up with a customer because they paid for the VIP treatment, but he wants a relationship, something I never, ever did. I don't shit where I eat, no matter that this is my business. But I can't say I'm not intrigued by Bartholomew. Just as he did his research on me, I definitely can't and won't make a decision until I did some thorough research on him.

"I need time to think about that. I can't give you an answer right away. Besides, I don't know shit about you. For all I know, you came here and fucked me with a dirty dick and now I'm infected. But that was dumb of me for even allowing shit to go down without protection."

"I told you I did my research on you. Do you honestly think I would have run up in you raw without knowing your situation, especially being that you work in a strip club? Shorty, I don't get down like that. Can't no bitch come up to you and truthfully say I gave her an STD or got her pregnant. I always strap up, but I didn't and don't want to do that with you. I know you clean, that's I ran up in you raw."

I sat up and punched his ass in his chest hard. It didn't have and affect on him though. He was shocked if anything that I hit him, but I didn't give a shit. "Nigga, are you purposely trying to get me pregnant?"

"Nah, but if it happens, I'm cool with it. But yo check it, don't be putting your hands on me like that. I don't hit women, but if you keep doing that shit to me, I'm gonna fuck you up." Bartholomew climbed out of bed and walked over to the table. He sat his bare ass on the sofa and snatched up the bottle of Hennessey. He didn't bother pouring any into a cup. He just poured it down his throat, taking huge gulps.

"I'm sorry. I shouldn't have hit you. But the way you came off was like you were trying to get me knocked up when you think you know me, but you don't. I won't do that again." I was now sitting on the side of the bed with my feet dangling.

Neither one of us spoke for several minutes, just sitting staring at each other. What is it about this strange man I allowed to penetrate me without protection? I'm calling Johnny first thing tomorrow to get his input. Family or no family, Johnny will keep it real with me and if Bartholomew wasn't what he was making himself out to be, Johnny wouldn't hesitate to tell me.

"Come here," he summoned me over to him.

I hopped off the bed and sauntered over to him. I straddled his legs and he leaned back against the sofa. I slowly leaned in and kissed his lips. They were soft. I tasted the Hennessey immediately. My eyes stayed open and, on his eyes, as I kissed him again. Bartholomew wrapped an arm around my waist and pulled me more into him, deepening our kiss. He opened his mouth and I inserted my tongue, sucking his top lip into mine. I moaned in his mouth as our tongues played a game of tag, chasing each other, sucking on each other's tongues and lips.

It was when Bartholomew lifted me up that I realized I had closed my eyes. When I opened them, he was staring at me with so much lust and passion. I felt my juices flow out of me. He rubbed the tip of his dick in my trickling juices before sliding me down on him until I had all of him inside of me. We both moaned in unison as we began to kiss again. After sitting on his dick a few minutes getting adjusted to him, I began to slowly ride him. I could feel him all the way in my stomach and couldn't get down like I would normally ride. He was just too damn big.

I wailed when Bartholomew hoisted me up then slammed me down on him. He did this several times and I whimpered more. I couldn't gather my words up to tell him how painful that was because just as quickly he began to fuck me from the bottom, and it started to feel just as good.

"Yes, just like that. Keep it like that," I told him. I wrapped my arms around his neck as he latched on to a breast. He sucked on my dark nipple, biting on it. It hardened more. He rolled the other nipple between his thumb and forefinger as he sucked on the other, then switching up. I arched my back and rode faster. It began to feel so good; I placed my hands on his knees behind me and leaned back. I rolled my hips back and forth, then twirled clockwise.

Bartholomew spread my legs apart further by opening his legs wider and leaning back against the sofa. I tossed my head back as I picked up the pace, fucking his massive dick. I started coming as soon as he rubbed his thumb on my clit. My pussy and stomach muscles clamped down so tight around him, that he began to come right behind me. Bartholomew guided me faster and harder on him as he skeeted inside of me. We both loudly moaned in pleasure as we rode the waves of our orgasms.

There were two knocks on the door indicating we had fifteen minutes before our time was up. I was happy and sad; happy because I was sore as fuck and there was no way I would be able to go a fourth round and sad because I honestly didn't want the night to end. I was still straddling his lap with his dick still inside me.

"We have fifteen minutes left," I told him.

"Oh yeah? We need to get cleaned up then. Shit I don't want the night to end here though. How about you come home with me?" Bartholomew asked.

"I can't tonight, but I can get up with you tomorrow," I replied. I have to make sure business was handled tonight since I wasn't out on the floor to see what went on. It's always my business before any dick, no matter how good that shit is.

"Cool, but in the meantime let me get one more in before our time is up," Bartholomew said. With that he picked me up and sat me on his face as he leaned against the sofa. His togue snaked inside my pussy and he ate my peach, sopping up all the juices as I came within a minute of his tongue action. He then placed me on my feet and had me lean over the arm of the sofa as he entered me from behind. He pumped in me hard and fast causing my feet to lift up off the floor.

"Ooh, shit! Shit!" I bawled out as I began to come again. Bartholomew put a hurting on my pussy as he slammed inside me for four more strokes before he released his load inside me. He fisted my hair as he came long and hard, not releasing me until he was empty.

He helped me up and we began to get dressed. He had just stuck his foot into his Timbs when Beast knocked then opened the door. "Times up," he informed us. Beast stood by the door waiting for us to exit. The entire time he scowled at Bartholomew.

Bartholomew ignored Beast and came over to me. He placed his hand on my waist, pulling me closer to him. I wrapped my arms around his neck, and we kissed. Our kiss deepened and he grabbed my ass squeezing my cheeks.

"Time's up," Beast belted out again. I pulled away from Bartholomew, breaking our kiss. I could feel his body tensing up and thought it was best to separate these two before they let their egos get the best of the them.

"Come on. Let's go. The club's getting ready to close," I grabbed Bartholomew by the hand and led him out of the room. Once we were in the hallway, I pecked his lips once more and promised to call him when I made it home from the club. He gave me his card and left out.

"What the hell is going on with you tonight, Beast?" I turned to him after Bartholomew was gone.

"Silky, that dude is trouble and it would best if you not fuck him anymore."

"Why? What's the tea on him, Beast? If you know something spill it and don't leave me hanging."

"Word on the street is that he was the one that killed Sam, then took over his operation. You know his wife Constance had that restaurant and hair salon, along with his auto shop over on Ninth Ave."

"Yeah, I heard she closed all of that down after Sam died."

"Correction, ya boy somehow snatched all of it right from under her and shut her down. Their building one of those condominiums with the shopping plaza on the bottom in that area. Look, I'm not trying to be in your business, but I'm doing my job and looking out for you. Before you make any more moves with dude, just make sure they're worth it." Beast walked off leaving me standing there with my thoughts.

I finally made it to the locker room where the ladies were winding down from the night's work. I went straight to the shower and hopped in. I heard bits and pieces of the chatter of them talking about me in the VIP room for the rest of the night. These dumb bitches always talking shit and worrying about the wrong thing, then I have to go in and school their asses on why I'm able to move like I do. I think it was becoming time I let everyone know who owns and runs this place, because the disrespect was getting out of hand.

I finished my shower and stepped out. I went over and sat at my vanity; I watched from my peripheral as the other ladies threw daggers my way. I brushed my hair in a ponytail then got dressed. Ken and DJ Domino came to the back for a quick roundup we always have at the end of the night. Beast came and grabbed the suitcase with my clothes and headed back out to wait for me at the bar.

"It's time," I said to Ken and DJ. They both looked surprised knowing what I meant when I said those two words. After the shock wore off, both men smiled then stood back and waited. Ms. Debra caught on and took a seat in the nearest chair since she knew the shit was about to hit the fan.

"Ladies, did y'all have a good night?" I asked. I looked around to each of the ladies, but no one said anything.

"Um, Ken, why is she talking? Don't nobody want to hear shit she has to say," Buffy, one of the ladies who had been at the club just about as long as I had been there, said.

"Well, Ladies, it's like this right here. She is the owner of this here establishment, which means I, as well as all of you, work for her," Ken said.

"That's bullshit! DJ Domino, what the fuck is going on?" Angel, a slim light-skinned chic asked.

"Exactly what Ken just said."

"Let me explain something to y'all. While some of you, nah most of you spending your money on bullshit, I was saving my money to invest in real shit like this club. When Johnny announced he was ready to retire from the business, I paid him cash for what we negotiated. DJ Domino has a piece in this club since he brought me on and helped me out when my momma kicked me out of the house over a bum ass nigga."

I walked around looking each one of the ladies in their eyes as I told them my story none of them ever knew. I broke it down to them the same way I tried to on several occasions to get them to understand the need to invest that money they make every night. Even though I was a major headliner for the club, lots of those ladies still bring in three thousand a week. Twelve grand a month is more than enough for them to make sound investments to get them out of this gritty world. Announcing that I was the owner of this club was my way of saying I was officially done stripping and was about to be about my future business endeavors.

"That's still some bullshit! So, you were in VIP with that nigga all this damn time what because you the boss and you just didn't want to dance or what? Honestly y'all just on some bullshit and I don't like it," Buffy said.

"You don't like it because he wasn't checking for you, bitch," Diamond said.

"Ladies, we not doing that tonight. Buffy, that man paid full price to have me in VIP for the remainder of the night so that's what he got. Now when you get a customer that is willing to pay full price for you in VIP for the whole night, by all means, do the damn thing. But at any rate, whether or not if I was in VIP, I still make money. Now can you say the same thing?'

Buffy's face turned red with rage. She couldn't say the same thing because she didn't have it like that. Even on the days I didn't work, she still never had it like that. And it wasn't that she was ugly or not shapely. No, Buffy was a pretty woman with a banging body. She just had a nasty aura about her that many people picked up on quickly and dismissed her just as quick.

"So, what does this mean since you're telling us this?" Ms. Debra asked.

"What is means is that I will no longer be dancing. Tonight, was going to be my last night as a dancer regardless of my VIP. I will be putting on my business owner hat and running the business. Ken will still be the manager so everyone will still report to him. DJ is still the deejay and Ms. Debra you are still the house mother. None of the staff is being replaced because you all do great jobs. Well most of you anyway. I think with some attitude adjustments the rest of you can survive, if not I'm not opposed to sending you on your way."

I looked directly at Buffy when I made that last statement. Oohs and uh-oh came from several people. My phone rang and I dismissed everyone for the night. They all scattered about packing up and heading out the door. I grabbed my phone and was about to answer when shots rang out towards the front of the club. Everyone began running towards the back door exit except for Ken, DJ, and me. We all pulled out guns and cocked the handles.

We eased towards the front where the shots were still coming from. My security detail was in a faceoff with Bartholomew and his goons. Fuck! I looked around for Beast but didn't see him anywhere.

"Punk motherfucka!" I heard someone say.

"Samyrah, get your ass out here before I kill your bitch ass bouncer!" Bartholomew shouted. Ken and DJ tried to get me to stay where it was at, but I had to remind them exactly who the fuck I was.

"So, is this how you do shit, Bartholomew?" I stepped out from behind out of the hallway and entered the main section of the club. When I got close to the bar, it was then I saw Beast laid out on the floor in a pool of his blood. I couldn't tell if he was still alive. I prayed he was, but it wasn't looking too good from my vantage point.

"Shorty, you know what's up. I'm here to collect what's rightfully mine," Bartholomew said breaking my train of thought.

"I'm sorry. What? What's rightfully yours?"

"This club and all the money you done made in the bitch. It's mine and I want it."

"You obviously done lost your fucking mind. I mean, I heard niggas going ape shit crazy after I put this bomb ass pussy on them, but until now I never knew how true it was," I laughed.

"Oh, don't flatter yourself, sweetheart. It was good, but it wasn't all that. Trust me, I've had better," Bartholomew said cockily.

"Yeah, you go right ahead and keep telling yourself that. Big B, I told you earlier you think you know me, but you don't. You are coming at me like this, shooting my men and shit. That's not how you go about getting my attention. I appreciate a man coming to me as a man instead of trying to handle me. During your research did you find out what happened to the last man that tried to handle me?"

"Nah I didn't but I can tell you that you been playing with these fuck niggas."

"So, your uncle didn't tell you my whole story huh?"

"Nah, I stopped listening to that motherfucka a long time ago. But since you so into storytelling, why don't you fill me in. I'm sure we would like to know," Bartholomew said sarcastically.

Pow! He never saw it coming as I pulled my gun from behind my waist and hole right in the center of his forehead. Bartholomew's body made a loud thud as it hit the floor lifeless. Beast was right about Bartholomew. However, I already knew who Bartholomew was when he stepped foot inside the Tasty Peach. Johnny, his very own uncle, called me and gave me the heads up and the greenlight to handle him as I saw fit to do so when the time came.

Yeah, I know this isn't the type of ending you were hoping for in this type of book, but this is it. People always tend to underestimate me because I'm a woman, and a loner. But what you should know is that when you try to play this pussy, it's you who will get fucked.

.... wait, wait, wait; I'm sorry y'all it actually didn't end that way. Turns out I did get pregnant by Bartholomew that night, but I miscarried a few weeks later. But I did get a new boo and we're doing just fine. Beast, or Brian as he likes me to call him now, survived his gun shot wounds. I helped nurse him back to health. He finally told me how he felt about me and hated the fact I slept with Bartholomew knowing what he knew about him. I knew something was up with him that night because he never acted that way before. But us spending time together as he recovered from his wounds opened up a side of him, sides of us that we never knew about each other.

Our relationship blossomed at the right time and when we finally made love, let me tell you I thought I was fucking with another Bartholomew because my bae is hung like a damn horse. Brian's just more in tune with my body and knowing how well-endowed he is, he takes his time with me and makes sure I don't faint! He feeds me the dick like only he can, and I love evry inch of it, of him, of us! I learned how to handle all that good vitamin D that's supplied by Brian.

As a matter of fact, telling y'all about it has me all hot and bothered. I'm about to hop off this and go hop on my man. I would give you a play by play but this right here is between the Beast and I. Smooches!

Coming Soon

DIVA YOLAN PRESENTS

A Diva's Revenge

Payback's a bitch

Yolanda Williams

YOLANDA WILLIAMS

Coming Soon

Diva Yolan Presents

Tantalizing Tales

Steaming *Scorching *Sweltering

Yolanda Williams

YOLANDA WILLIAMS

About the Author

Yolanda Williams was born in Columbus, MS and is third of four children. As a child, she always had an imagination and talent for writing. It wasn't until later as an adult she decided to pursue her writing talent and with that her first novel Bounded by Love was created. Yolanda now resides in Lithonia, GA.

www.ingramcontent.com/pod-product-compliance
Lightning Source LLC
Chambersburg PA
CBHW031947240626
47153CB00003B/893